MINDERS

Diana Hendry is a poet and the author of numerous stories for young readers, including *Harvey Angell*, Winner of the 1991 Whitbread Children's Novel Award. Among her other titles for young readers are the picture books *Dog Dottington* and *Christmas in Exeter Street* and the chapter books *Fiona Says…*; *Sam Sticks and Delilah*; *Wonderful Robert and Sweetie-pie Nell*; *Flower Street Friends* and *Midnight Pirate, Midnight Party*. She is also the author of a novel for older readers, *Double Vision*, and two volumes of poetry, one for adults and one for children. Although she does not possess any magical powers like the young wizard Scully in *Minders*, she does have a minor talent for spinning plates!

D1589767

MINDERS

DIANA HENDRY

WALKER BOOKS
AND SUBSIDIARIES
LONDON · BOSTON · SYDNEY

First published 1998 by Walker Books Ltd
87 Vauxhall Walk, London SE11 5HJ

This edition published 1999

2 4 6 8 10 9 7 5 3 1

Text © 1998 Diana Hendry
Cover illustration © 1998 Mark Preston

This book has been typeset in Sabon.

Printed in Great Britain by Cox & Wyman Ltd, Reading, Berkshire

British Library Cataloguing in Publication Data
A catalogue record for this book is available from
the British Library.

ISBN 0-7445-6940-0

For Vivian and Isobel – with love

CONTENTS

THE SECRET

I never tell anyone. About my dad being a Wizard I mean. Well, you can imagine what people would say, can't you? Things like, "Oh yeah, and my dad's King Kong."

It's not exactly against the rules. To tell, I mean. Dad just says it's unwise. Unwise is my dad's favourite word. Cars are *unwise* according to my dad and telephones that play jingles at you. I've known my dad decide not to get up in the morning and when anyone asks him why, he just says "Unwise! Unwise!" in a deeply gloomy voice. Perhaps he knows it's going to rain all day or that there's going to be a bomb scare in town. But I don't think so.

It's my mum who's the Seer. Not an all-the-time Seer, just a sometimes-Seer. She likes to call herself a "figure-caster", which means that she tells fortunes. It's a better career than Wizardry. You can earn a living telling fortunes whereas my dad never made a penny out of being a Wizard.

When people ask me what my dad does, I say, "He works in the market. He's got the clock stall." Which is true. And I *don't* go on to tell them, "but his really serious job is Wizardry," or that I'm what's known as a Wizard-in-waiting. That's what you are before you qualify. The waiting is awful. And uncomfortable. Sometimes I think it's what hatching must feel like to a chicken inside an egg. It knows it's got legs and wings but it can't yet stretch them. If you're a Wizard-in-waiting you know you've got all kinds of Powers growing inside you. Hatching. Anyway, in my case it looked as if the waiting might go on for ages because all of a sudden I got a Minder.

Jed Sullivan – he's the nearest I've got to a best mate – says you have to be mad, bad, very thick or very lucky to get a Minder. "Statemented" the teachers call it, which sounds as if they've pinned a notice on your back saying THIS BOY NEEDS WATCHING. We call it "getting a Minder", because that's what actually happens. I got a Minder because I'd been off school a lot. Viruses, the doctor said, and very strange viruses too, the like of which he'd never known.

Dad and I knew it was just that I was coming into my Powers. It's a known fact that coming into your Powers can make you feel very odd. It's like some bits of you are growing too fast. There isn't space in your mind for things like schoolwork. And sometimes you get a kind of Flash as if you've seen into another world. Then it's gone and you can't remember it properly. Except you know it was important. Anyway, try telling Miss Pugh – she's our headteacher – any of that.

"Scully," she said, (everyone calls me that, even my parents though my proper name is Erasmus. Erasmus Browne. My mother chose Erasmus because the name means *lovely* and *deserving of love*, which was the first thing she thought after I was born. But I got the name Scully because before I could walk I used to "scull" my way over the floor on my bum using my arms as oars.) Anyway, "Scully," said Miss Pugh, "it's not just that you've missed a lot of classes, it's also that when you *are* in class, you seem to go off in a day-dream. And you don't seem to appreciate that you haven't got all the time in the world. When everyone else is finishing, you're just beginning."

I wanted to explain to Miss Pugh that she was quite wrong. I *did* have all the time in the world. I can never quite believe how the People-people (as compared to us Wizard folk) have got Time so wrong. They don't seem to know about the Present-Eternal and they don't understand that dreaming is work. But of course I couldn't say any of this.

"We'd never get our work done if people knew about us," Dad had told me years ago. "The People-people are funny about magic. They want it. Oh they want it badly, but they are also afraid of it. Magic's like love. Powerful stuff. So you must always do your best to pass for normal, Scully – like your mother and I do."

Now if you ask me, my parents don't always do too well at passing for normal, but they try hard. So I don't like to tell Dad that forgetting to take off his Wizard's Hat when he puts the dustbins out isn't exactly "normal". And I don't point out to Mum that telling the bus driver that she can See a distant relative coming to visit him, isn't something many mothers do.

Anyway, as I couldn't tell Miss Pugh any of this, I fixed my eyes on the rather skinny spider plant growing on her desk. I know I shouldn't practise certain Wizard skills yet – not until I'm fully into my Powers – but I couldn't resist seeing if I could encourage it a little. It looked so pathetic and struggling.

"Scully!" said Miss Pugh. "Will you please look at me when I'm talking to you. And listen! We have arranged that Ms Brewer will be your Minder. She will attend certain lessons with you and check that you've done your homework and help you with any problems.

You're to come to my office at break tomorrow and I'll introduce you. So be sure you're there – and *on time*! Understood?"

"Yes, miss," I said.

"And Scully..." said Miss Pugh as I got to the door, "no magic tricks."

"No, miss," I said. I could see her looking at the spider plant as I closed the door behind me. It had grown an extra frond or two. I thought it looked distinctly happier. But what had she meant, Miss Pugh, with her "no magic tricks"? She couldn't know, could she? I decided it was just one of those chance remarks People-people make without guessing it might be true.

Anyway, Miss Pugh wasn't my problem. Ms Brewer was. How was I going to cope with a Minder watching over me? How was I going to get the Dreaming done and my Changing Practice? And I didn't think Dad was going to be too pleased about it either. I thought I'd better go and find him down in the market.

WHAT O'CLOCK?

I like the market. It's in a big echoey hall – at least it's echoey when the stall holders have packed up and gone home. Late afternoon it's busy and noisy. I like it much better than the supermarket where Mum sometimes drags me to push the trolley and help pack the boxes.

The market where Dad works is all jumbly and untidy and that makes it exciting. And you never quite know what you're going to find. There's everything there – old books, masks and jokes, toys, cheeses, fish, jewellery, hats – and of course my dad with his clocks and watches. The stall holders aren't in uniform either, like they are in the supermarket. They wear what they like. In winter they're all bundled up in coats and scarves or layers of jerseys because it can get very cold in the market. That's because the roof's made of glass. You can look up and see clouds floating by and pigeons looking down at you. Anyway the *feeling* in the market isn't cold. It's warm and friendly and comforting.

I found my dad doing surgery on an old carriage clock. He had all its insides laid out tidy on a long piece of purple velvet. Cogs, tiny gold screws, little wheels with edges like a saw, curls of wire. I sat down on a stool beside him.

"This clock," said my dad, "might have known Queen Victoria or possibly it might have sat on Darwin's mantelpiece and ticked its way through *On the Origin of Species*. I expect it was very helpful."

That's the way my dad is about clocks. A clock's like a history book to my dad and history's his Thing. I suppose it has to be, really, seeing that he's a Class Three Wizard. Perhaps I should explain. There're Wizards of the Past, Present and Future. Dad looks after Times Past (Class Three). That means he has to find and rescue Ancient Knowledge. Dad says there's a lot of this all over the place, that people are very careless. They decide something's no use so they throw it out or put it away – in the back of their minds or cupboards – and then everyone forgets about it. According to Dad there was someone before Copernicus who thought the Earth went round the Sun, only whoever-it-was lost the stone on which he'd scribbled his sums.

Personally I think Dad spends too *much*

time in Times Past. It makes him gloomy. I've seen him, when the market's quiet, sitting there twiddling his moustache with one hand and turning back the fingers of a clock as if he was winding Time the wrong way. But he won't hear a word said against Times Past.

"Without the past," my dad says, "the present is like a white sauce without an onion. Why?" (Dad always answers his own questions, so I don't bother.) "Because the onion gives the sauce its flavour."

Dad was looking reasonably cheerful but all the same I waited until he'd put the carriage clock together again. Even so, I thought he was going to drop the clock on the floor when I said, "I've got a Minder, Dad. Miss Pugh has given me a Minder."

"A Minder?" growled Dad. "What do you want with a Minder when you've got your mum and me – not to mention the Outlandish Gentry?" (The Outlandish Gentry is the West Country Branch of the Wizards.)

"Miss Pugh says I've missed a lot of school and I do too much day-dreaming. The Minder's going to come to lessons with me and check up on homework and I've to see her if I've any problems. Her name's Ms Brewer."

I said this all in a rush. I do this when something's difficult to say – as if saying it very fast will make the other person swallow it quickly. Not that it worked on Dad.

"Msssss Brewer!" he said, making the Ms buzz like a bee. "*She's* the problem!" And he began packing away the stall as if there was no Time (past, present or future) to lose.

"A Minder indeed!" he went on. "Sounds more like a Snooper to me. She'll cause no end of trouble. Delay everything. Just when you're coming into your Powers and the Outlandish Gentry will need you."

"I don't think it will be so bad," I said doubtfully. (Actually I was really curious about Ms Brewer.) "I'm sure I'll manage. I'm meeting her at break tomorrow."

"How are you going to get your Dreaming done?" demanded Dad. "Minimum ten hours a week, remember. And how are you going to practise your Changing?"

"Maybe when she's not looking," I said miserably. We'd begun putting the clocks away in the locked cases Dad keeps under the stall. All of them go in the cases except for the grandfather clock.

The grandfather clock *looks* as if it's for sale. But it isn't. Whenever I ask Dad about it he gets all mysterious and says, "I'm looking after it for someone."

"Who?" I ask.

"You'll see," he says. And that's as far as we get. The grandfather's never wound up either and Dad keeps its pendulum in a special black velvet glove. Whenever we leave the market

Dad gives the grandfather a pat and says, "good drop of Eternity in that clock," which, for a clock that never ticks or tocks seems to me a very funny thing to say. But I try to be tolerant. All parents have their funny ways.

"This Minder of yours," said Dad "will be looking at everything from your haircut to your homework. I might have to vamoosh her."

I felt quite scared then. Dad's not the sort of Wizard who vamooshes people. And nowadays vamooshing is against Wizard law. "I don't think you should vamoosh her," I said nervously. "I think Miss Pugh might notice."

"Maybe I'd better come with you to meet her then," said Dad. "I could shiver her a little. Just put her off. Suggest she go and mind someone else. Lordy lord!" he shouted, waving his arms wide and startling the last few shoppers. "There're loads of people in need of minding. Why you?"

I didn't answer that. But I managed to persuade Dad *not* to come with me to meet Ms Brewer. I didn't want him around trying to "pass for normal" and looking outrageous. No. I thought I'd try to deal with Ms Brewer by myself. I just hoped she was a careless sort of Minder.

CHANGING PRACTICE

I don't know why, but somehow I imagined a Minder would be about ninety – a kind of very grey and grim granny. Ms Brewer was nothing like that. She was young. Young enough to be wearing a miniskirt and boots. And she had a mop of ginger hair.

I knew Miss Pugh wasn't too happy with her because before I knocked at her office door, I stopped to listen. Yes, yes, I know I shouldn't have done but it wasn't as if I'd *chosen* to have a Minder was it? Do Minders look after your mind, I was wondering as I listened at the door. Well, I was planning to look after my own.

"You do look frightfully young," I heard Miss Pugh say, "and we felt that Scully needed someone – someone mature, someone with two feet on the ground."

I heard Ms Brewer laugh. "Well, I was

specially chosen for Scully," she said, "and I do assure you that my feet are very firmly on the ground."

"Specially chosen?" By whom, I wondered. But I knocked at the door then and Miss Pugh called me in.

The trouble with Miss Pugh is that her magic gene's never been activated. The state of a person's magic gene is something every trainee Wizard learns about. Everyone's got a magic gene but some people never find it, or they neglect it. According to my mum it's the magic gene that makes people open or closed. "A person with a good working magic gene rings like a fine glass when you tap it," says Mum. "And a person with an idle magic gene just makes a kind of dull ting."

Miss Pugh was making a very dull ting that morning. I could tell from her face that she'd already made up *her* mind that Ms Brewer was not the right Minder.

"Scully," she said, "this is Ms Brewer. I've given her your past reports and some of your work books. You could spend the next period in the library getting to know each other. I'd like to think you could establish a nice quiet routine." I suppose there was something about Ms Brewer's wild ginger hair that made you think a "quiet routine" rather unlikely. But Ms Brewer just smiled very politely at Miss Pugh, crossed her sheeny legs and said, "Scully

22

will be safe in my hands, Miss Pugh."

Off we went to the library, leaving Miss Pugh looking particularly glum. Actually she didn't need to worry. I could almost see a speech bubble over Ms Brewer's bright head which said *Minder in Action*. She set about it at once, snapping open her briefcase and spreading my reports and work books over the library table.

Then she looked at me. Her eyes were the colour of treacle toffee, dark, deep and – well, knowing. Looking into her eyes was like being given a hug.

"As from this moment, Scully," she said, "I'm going to keep close tabs on you. Very close tabs."

I think I gave a rather weak smile. I mean it was nice the way she looked at me as if she really cared about me. But "close tabs" – that sounded as if she planned to keep her treacle eyes on me twenty-four hours a day. Then there was that mop of wild ginger hair. If you bumped into Ms Brewer in the street you'd think, at first, that she was just a trendy young thing. Until you got to the hair. It wasn't just the colour. It was the amazing frizz of it. I think if you touched it you might get an electric shock. I didn't plan on trying.

"Well now," she said, as if she'd learnt all she needed to know with one long brown look, "these reports..." and she dived into them like a bird dive-bombing a snail. She pushed one across to me. "A bit worrying, don't you think?"

Scully seems to spend a lot of time twisting himself into strange shapes, I read, *and very little time doing the maths problems set him*.

I had to grin a little at that because I remembered how I'd just begun my Changing Exercises and it was all so fascinating that I couldn't wait until I was at home to try one or two out.

The Changing Exercises are probably stage one of a Wizard's education. Wizards – trainee Wizards like me – don't learn *about* things. They *become* things. I mean, a biology lesson for a Wizard wouldn't be learning *about* ants, it would be turning *into* one. I've done this once during a Practice and it was very tricky. Or maybe I should say sticky because I nearly ran into a great pool of sweet ant-killing syrup. I got one of my legs stuck and could have drowned if I hadn't realized just in time and changed back into myself. I've got a tiny peeled spot on my little toe as a reminder of that. It's much more fun, and less hard work, turning into a woodlouse and trundling about like a miniature tank. Ants are tribal and work terribly hard. The woodlouse is slow and thoughtful.

Anyway, the thing about the Changing Exercises is that you have to learn the knack of remembering yourself. I suppose that sounds rather daft. But it's easy, in the excitement of Changing, to get carried away and forget who you are. Or were. And then you can't get back into yourself. So it's all very dangerous. My mum says there's a price for Wizardly powers and it's not being properly grounded. Not having your feet on the ground. She's got a special herbal medicine that she doses me with which is meant to help. My dad just tells warning tales about Wizards who changed into trees or hens or worms and couldn't get back again.

As far as I know it's all quite different for People-people. They have trouble forgetting themselves. I often think this must get exceptionally tiring, being yourself all the time. I had that feeling about Ms Brewer – that she couldn't ever escape herself; that she always knew who she was and where she was and what she was. I almost felt sorry for her. But you couldn't really feel sorry for someone who had as much brightness about her as Ms Brewer had.

I'd rather drifted off into all these thoughts, sitting opposite her at the library table on that first meeting, and it was only when she reached over and tweaked my nose that I came to again and found myself looking at the report for sports which said simply, *The most useless goalkeeper I have ever known.*

That was hardly fair, I thought. It had been a wonderfully sunny spring day when Mr Tovey made me goalkeeper, and there were all sorts of distractions. Things you might Change yourself into. Blossom. Swallows. A waking tortoise.

"One way and another," Ms Brewer said, "it's not a very good record is it, Scully?"

"No, miss," I said.

"Monika," she said. "You can call me Monika. I'm not a teacher, you know. And I hope we'll become friends. Now I think it might be a very good idea if we arranged a meeting with your parents. Then we can have a Plan of Action and know we're all pulling together. What d'you think?"

What I thought was that Plans of Action were what Ms Brewer – Monika – liked best of all. But I was feeling very wide awake now. I had an instant picture of my dad saying "Unwise! Unwise!" In fact I said it out loud, shaking my head just like he does.

"Unwise! Unwise!" I said.

Monika looked faintly surprised. Her hair seemed to frizz with so much static it almost crackled. Then she laughed. "I know how it is," she said. "School life and home life – often you don't want the two put together. But I think in this case it would be very wise. Very wise indeed. We can all work out how you can catch up on your schoolwork. I'm sure there's a lot you can achieve if I keep an eye on you. Shall we say four o'clock Thursday? After school?"

She didn't give me time to say yes or no. And anyway, it wasn't really a question. She swept all the reports together, snapped shut her briefcase, gazed into my eyes once more as if to confirm whatever it was she'd seen there first time, and said, "Thursday then, Scully. I shall look forward to it. I'm sure you have a very interesting family."

HATS, CLOAKS AND ACTION PLANS

"Interesting!" groaned my dad when I told him. He was wearing his Wizard's Hat when I got home. I knew what that meant. He was preparing himself for a visit to Times Past. The Hat's a really traditional job – black and pointed and with embroidered gold stars. I hate it. "Why can't you be more original? More trendy?" I've often asked him. To which my dad always says, "I'm quite original enough, thank you very much and I like to have something about my person that is part of the tradition." I think the Hat was his grandfather's or maybe his great-grandfather's. The point is it's *historical*. And battered. Several of the stars are missing and the peak is slightly squashed.

"It'll belong to you one day," my dad says.

"You'll never catch me wearing it," I say.

"I think you're both making far too much

fuss about this woman," said my mum, coming into the kitchen. "All we've got to do is pass for normal."

Dad and I both burst out laughing at this. You'd have to see the kitchen to understand why. Spell books instead of cook books. Astrological charts on the wall. A large bottle by the sink labelled *Scully's Grounding Medi.* Dad's equally awful matching Wizard's Cloak pegged on the back door.

Apart from this, the kitchen is rather bright. There are two purple walls and two yellow walls and Mum's made lampshades with cut-out patterns in them that throw shadows on the walls. One of them looks just like a rabbit.

"Well, we can clear some of this away," said Mum defensively. "Make it look ordinary."

"*Un*interesting," said Dad. "That's the effect we're after. *Un*interesting."

It took us almost all of Wednesday night making the house look *un*interesting. Mum drew the line at repainting the walls. We took down the portrait of my grandfather (in The Hat, of course) and put up a Matisse poster instead, and Mum put away her tarot cards and we rolled up the magic rug that has all kinds of ancient Wizard stories woven into it.

Dad objected to this. "It's not as if she's going to get down on her hands and knees and *read* it," he said.

"Better safe than sorry," said Mum. "You

want to be *un*interesting – *un*interesting we shall be." And she put down a dull grey mat in place of the magic rug.

The only part of the house we didn't have to worry about was the front. The front of the house is part of our passing-for-normal act. All you see from the outside is a very ordinary semi-detached house with net curtains at the windows and a fairly neat garden with a weeded path and a pot of geraniums – a rather fulsome pot (Mum waters it with a special brew) – to the left of the front door.

Of course if you looked very carefully you might notice a rather odd TV aerial, which is really attached to Dad's Telepod. (It catches scraps of knowledge from the Ancient World and taps them out on Dad's computer and then Dad has to decide what needs further investigation.)

Dad hates the computer. Some nights I can hear him shouting at it. "Once upon a time," says Dad – that's one of his favourite phrases – "we Wizards used to work by telepathy. Now we've lost the art." If you ask me, Dad would prefer pigeon post to the computer. Me? I think technology's just a new kind of magic.

The only strange thing about the garden is Mum's washing line. It's one of those whirligig things. Only Mum's has a little electro-magnetic chip at the end of each spoke. They're for picking up the vibes, she says. And when I ask her *what* vibes, she gets evasive and says it's something called the *Zeitgeist*. She gets a bit mystic, my mum, now and again. Personally I think the *Zeitgeist* is a kind of ghost with zits. But I haven't told her this. I don't think she'd be amused. Mum's sense of humour is very variable. Understanding is her big thing. It can get you down, Mum's understanding. Particularly when she sits you at the kitchen table and gets all big eyed and says, "Explain yourself! I just want to understand you, Scully!" She always seems to say this just at the time when I don't understand myself (i.e. most of the time). So there's no possible way I can "explain" myself.

Mum being a Seer, you'd think she'd be able to See into me without asking. But it doesn't work like that. Close family are excluded, she says. She can only do her Seeing and fortune-telling with people she's not attached to. That's why she can't See her own future either. It's a great pity. It would be really useful to know, but Mum says it's a protection, a *kind* protection, to those with the Gift.

Anyway, on that Thursday afternoon when I brought Ms Brewer – Monika – home, it was quite windy and Mum had a lot of washing on her whirligig. I thought this was a bit unwise because I could see some of Dad's travelling gear pegged there. (He has to have clothes for

Times Past, so he won't look out of place.) Also the whirligig made a little buzzing noise as we walked past so that Monika paused and looked all about her. Fortunately Mum was already at the door.

Mum had gone rather overboard about looking ordinary. She had the telly on and her knitting out. (Monika wasn't to know she only knitted blankets for Wizards in reduced circumstances.) The electric fire was on, though Dad usually just lights the real fire with a snap of his fingers like the person in the old gas ad.

Hardly were we inside when Dad arrived home from the market. Dad has more difficulty than Mum about looking normal. I think it's something to do with his green Wizard eyes and the way his moustache curls up at the ends.

"This is Ms Brewer," I said.

"Monika," said Ms Brewer. "Do call me Monika."

I could tell they were all rather surprised by each other. I saw Mum close her eyes for a moment as if dazzled by Monika's ginger hair. Dad, who's about mid-nineteenth century in his head, hurriedly put on his cardigan as if he needed something old (the cardigan's certainly that) and comforting about him.

As for Monika, well she looked seriously disappointed. Mum had succeeded in making everything, including herself, look very drab.

The whole room had a grey look. Monika gave a small sigh as if so much greyness depressed her. I could almost see her beginning to write her Minder's Report on Home Background. I felt rather sorry we'd changed everything. And I felt sure that Dad had already dismissed Monika as a *modern young thing*. Perhaps it was that which brought about the Flash.

A Flash is like a sudden insight into a person's true self. This one was really odd. I saw Monika dancing in a swirling blue robe like someone out of a Greek myth, her hair like a halo about her head. Then the Flash was over, and Monika was sitting there with a notepad on her miniskirted knees, smiling over-brightly at Mum.

Mum and Dad were being all outwardly respectful and polite. I didn't need a Flash to know they were like two tigers protecting their young, ready to pounce if Monika should put a well-polished boot wrong. Possibly Monika was used to tigerish parents because she began cautiously.

"I do hope you won't find me intrusive," she said. "A Minder's job…"

"A Snooper's job." I heard Dad mutter under his breath.

Monika pretended not to have heard, "is to be helpful, not interfering. Now Scully is obviously intelligent and imaginative but…"

I could almost see the tiger fur standing on

end with that "but" and I knew already that this was going to be one of those conversations in which I was talked about as if I wasn't there.

"But?" prompted Dad icily.

"But – well let's just say his imagination seems to run away with him a little," Monika said. You could tell she was falling over herself trying to be tactful and you could tell it was a strain. The ginger frizz fizzed a centimetre. "You could say he lives in a bit of a dream," she said, and laughed.

"*You* could say that," said Dad. "I'd just say he was stretching himself."

"Oh yes, stretching," said Monika hastily, as if, maybe, I was a piece of chewing gum, "but we want to see him stretching in all directions don't you think? Using all his abilities. Perhaps I should say in a *balanced* sort of way. It's really so important for Scully's future that he does well at school."

"We know about his future," said Dad. (I think if he could have roared, he would have done.) "Scully's going to be—"

But Mum jumped in. "It's just that Scully is going to inherit his father's clock stall in the market," she said. "He'll take over."

Monika's ginger eyebrows rose. "Ah, yes," she said, looking down at her notepad. "I was told something about a special inheritance."

Dad's eyebrows rose at that. (His are big and black and almost meet across his nose.)

He gave me a look as if to ask, *Have you been talking?* I shook my head. The word "special" rang bells in my head. It reminded me of Monika saying she'd been "specially chosen" to be my Minder.

"Well," Monika continued, "I hope Scully will have a choice in his future. The days are rather past when parents told their children exactly what they were going to do, don't you think?"

It was bravely said and I was about to say that I thought she was quite right, only my dad got in first. He was rather red in the face now.

"Scully will do what he's born to do," he said, in something like a growl.

"Then he'll need to be prepared," said Monika rather sharply.

"I think that's up to me," said Dad.

Monika sighed and soothed down her miniskirt. Clearly she thought she'd met an ancient Victorian tyrant and would have to make the best of things. My mum had gone very quiet. I knew by the misty look she had that she'd gone off into her Seer's mode.

What with Dad getting all growly and Mum all misty, I thought Monika was having a very hard time. Not that I was on her side. I didn't much care for all those sweet "don't you's" she seemed to tag on to the end of her sentences, as if she wanted to bully you into agreeing with her.

Monika sat up very straight and said, "Let's forget about the future for the moment and concentrate on the here-and-now." (You could tell the here-and-now was where she was most at home.) "An Action Plan," she said. "Now, I've a list here of the subjects in which Scully has fallen behind. If it were possible for him to do an extra half-hour's homework during this term, I'm sure he could catch up." She turned appealingly to my mum. "Perhaps you could help him with that? Fix a time he can really settle down to work."

"Scully's got all his Changing—" Dad began.

"I'm sure I could do that," said Mum very sweetly. She was looking at Monika quite differently, I thought, as if she'd seen something we didn't know about.

"I shall be happy to mark his work," said Monika, "and of course I shall be helping him in class. Making sure his attention doesn't wander."

"Wandering. Wondering." said Dad, "That's what he's meant to be doing."

"Tea," said Mum. "I'm sure Ms Brewer would like some tea."

"Thank you, but no," said Monika. "I really must be getting home. I'll see you tomorrow, Scully. Period one."

We all went out into the hall. I was just fetching Monika's mac from the cupboard where Mum had hung it when Dad's Hat – hidden on the top shelf with the ordinary scarves and gloves – fell out.

"Oh!" said Monika, as if after all the greyness she was rather pleased to see something that shone. There was a long silence. Then, "Fancy dress!" said Monika. And before anyone could say a word she did something totally unexpected. She picked up the Hat and put it on her head.

Now that Hat has sort of grown magic powers of its own. Having been on at least two, possibly three, Wizard heads, you could say it's soaked in magic.

We all stood staring silently at Monika standing in our hall in my dad's Hat. She twisted it a little on her head and then looked at herself in the cupboard mirror. Her ginger hair frizzed as if it was about to catch fire.

"D'you know, I think I feel a little dizzy," said Monika.

Mum whisked the Hat off her head. "Better sit down and have that cup of tea," she said.

"Yes, yes, I think I will," said Monika.

"Even Minders need minding sometimes," said Mum and she gave me a wink.

ABOUT THE OUTLANDISH GENTRY

Lying in bed that night, I thought a lot about Monika saying children should be free to choose their futures. It stuck in my head because if you're a Wizard-in-waiting you don't *have* a choice. And who'd want one, given the magic powers and adventures of a Wizard's life?

Mostly I wouldn't want things to be any different. Mostly. In fact there's only one thing wrong with being a Wizard-in-waiting. It's lonely. There's not many of us, and you can never quite belong to the People-people. You can't talk to them about Changing into an ant or being on a quest for Ancient Knowledge or having a Flash because if you did they'd probably lock you up. It's possible, I sometimes think, that Wizardry is a dying profession. I'm the only trainee in the West Country Branch of the Outlandish Gentry. The East Country has two, the North three and the South one.

There's a girl in my class – Lizzie Moreland – who has very rich parents. Having money is a bit like having magic powers, I sometimes think, and that's why Lizzie's lonely. I don't know why her parents have sent her to our school instead of one of those expensive boarding schools with miles of grounds.

I like Lizzie – and I feel sorry for her. You can tell she tries hard not to talk about their five cars and their holiday home in Tuscany and weekend breaks in New York. And I think she has quite a hard time trying to look a bit scruffy like the rest of us. Probably cuts the designer labels off her clothes. Lizzie could really do with a Minder, but no one would dream of giving her one because she's a girl who's got Too Much. I don't suppose anyone thinks having Too Much can cause as many problems as having Too Little. I guess they're different and more comfortable problems, but problems all the same.

Anyway, the point is, Lizzie doesn't talk about money and I don't talk about magic. Perhaps that's why I'm writing about it. Though what I'm going to do with all this, I don't know. Maybe bury it somewhere so that a Wizard of the future will find it when it's become Ancient, or Lost Knowledge. Or in case Wizards become extinct.

I suppose I was thinking all this too because

after Monika had gone Dad sat me down and said never mind about *Monika's* Plan of Action, we need one of our own.

It seems my Test by the Outlandish Gentry could happen almost any day now. Dad hadn't told me before because he didn't want me to get stressed out by it. The Test's in five parts, apparently:

1. To show you can Change into another Being of your own choice.
2. To show you can Change into another Being of the Examiner's choice.
3. To return (gracefully) into yourself.
4. To demonstrate a Flash.
5. To recite, from memory, the Wizard's Two-way Code.

As Dad pointed out, I wasn't nearly ready for all of this. Returning into myself, for instance, gives me an awful lot of trouble. It's like getting into a set of clothes that don't quite fit you. Certainly I can't do it *gracefully*.

As for the Flash, that sudden seeing into the heart of someone or something – well, that's happened *to* me (as when I saw Monika dancing in a blue robe) but I can't yet *make* a Flash happen. It needs a lot of very still, quiet concentration and practice.

Anyway, as Dad said, with Ms Brewer doing her snooping ... ("minding," I said. "Oh, all right, minding," said Dad) there

wasn't much time. I'd have to do all my practising at home.

"We can't afford to have her suspecting,"
said Dad. "You know what that would mean,
don't you?"

"Yes," I said, "we'd have to move. And
move fast. I wouldn't mind."

"Well *we* would!" said Dad.

I would mind, really, but I said that because
I was feeling a bit angry with him. I'd begun to
think it might be quite nice having a Minder.
Someone taking an interest in ordinary life, in
school life. Not that Mum and Dad don't, of
course. But they're both so busy – Dad with his
clocks and Times Past and Mum with her fortune telling and Times Future. But Monika's
sort of new. She's new and Now and exciting.

Also, I *did* want to do well at school. I'm
very competitive. Secretly I'd like to be top of
the class in everything. I'd certainly like to beat
Jed Sullivan and Lizzie Moreland.

Anyway, *Dad's* Plan of Action was that I
should get up extra early to do my Wizard
Training and then when I went to school I
should sort of switch off from it all. It sounded
to me like two sets of homework. Wizard
work and schoolwork. Early and late.

I told Dad I'd try. Well what choice did I
have? I suppose he's well practised in switch-
ing off and on. It's a rare occasion when Dad
resorts to his Wizard tricks in the market. He

once put a spell on someone who was about to nick a watch. It was quite a quiet spell. He just froze the man's right hand. The stealing hand. You could see the terrible fright in the man's face. He tried to shake the life back into his hand but he couldn't do it. The hand was turning blue and purple when Dad released it and asked him, very politely, if there was anything he wanted to buy. The man didn't even stop to answer. He just fled from the market. I expect he went straight to the doctor's.

And there was another time when a stray dog came into the market – all thin and hungry and going round the stalls hoping for scraps. Dad just sat back on his stool and closed his eyes. Next thing you knew the dog was attached to a lead and trotting along with a very nice mumsy sort of woman. She looked rather surprised to find herself with a dog. But he was a nice friendly sort of dog and he wagged his tail at her, so she just shrugged, gave him a pat and off they went together. They looked as if they might live happily ever after.

But mostly when Dad's in the market he's a clock man, not a Wizard. Most of his Wizard work's done at night. It involves a lot of reading and sometimes a bit of Time Travel. That's one of the things you can look forward to as a Class Three Wizard. You get to travel. The occasional quick whizz (wizz – ha-ha!) back to the tenth century perhaps, just to check a few things out. Research, my dad calls it, though if you ask me, when Dad finds the twentieth century more than he can take, he invents a bit of research.

My mum's always nagging to go with him but he always makes the same excuse. She hasn't got the right clothes. Mum says if he told her what they were, she could make them, couldn't she? Then he changes tack and says there's a language barrier too and can she speak Anglo-Saxon or Latin and Mum has to admit she can't.

When Dad had finished his lecture on How to Succeed in Wizardry by Really Trying, I had just enough time to catch Mum before she fell asleep on the sofa – which she often does at night. Seeing wears her out. I wanted to know what she'd Seen of Monika.

"Dancing," said Mum with one of her dreamy smiles. "I saw her dancing in a swirling blue robe. It was an important dance."

"Important for what?" I asked.

"I don't know," said Mum. "Important to the minding, I think."

"Is that all?" I asked. "Nothing more *useful*?"

"That *was* useful to me," said Mum. "I felt a lot better about her."

Of course I was impressed that Mum had

Seen Monika dancing just as I'd seen her in my Flash, but I'd been hoping that Mum had seen something really interesting. What I was most curious about was what I'd overheard Monika say to Miss Pugh. "I was specially chosen for Scully," she'd said. By who? That's what I wanted to know. And that's what I hoped Mum might have Seen – the person or persons who had "specially chosen" Monika to be my Minder. I should have known better. Mum's Seeing is often full of good signs or bad signs and that's as far as it goes.

I thought I'd just have to find out for myself.

MOANY DRONES

I quite like the look of my school. There's
something a bit fantastical about it, as though
the man who built it (who happens to be
William Larkins Bernard. I know because
Monika told me) got a bit bored. Every time
he reached the top of a wall he thought he'd
add an extra bit, a kind of camel's hump with
a bobble on top. He got really carried away
with his humps and bobbles (they're called
gables) so there are lots and lots of them – low
ones and high ones, big ones and little ones –
and the whole building is topped by a bell
tower and a weather vane. From a distance,
and against the sky, it looks wonderfully
nutty. William Larkins Bernard liked port-
holes too, so there are quite a lot of them. Perhaps he hoped the school might sail away like
Noah's ark, or like a Loch Ness Monster with
just its humps showing above water.

It's all rather different inside. The school's on four floors. On two of them there's a big hall in the middle and classrooms all round the sides. There are two staircases and a one-way system so you're meant to go up one and down the other, to avoid crashes. But people forget.

We're always moving rooms and having to lug our bags around and as the numbering of the rooms doesn't seem to be very logical (twenty is next to thirty-five) you have a hard job remembering where you're meant to be. Unless, of course, you're like Jed or Lizzie. Jed's got an amazing memory and Lizzie has the timetable Sellotaped to the flap of her bag. For myself, I have to look around and see who's heading where. So I just about made it on time to room thirty-five where we were having double music and where Monika was waiting at the door. She was all sheeny legs and polished boots. I think she'd just washed her hair because it looked like a firework display.

For the last few weeks we've been doing this very dull music project with Mr Jones (otherwise known as Moany Drones). We're learning about composers. At least that's the idea. I can't say it's the sort of music most of the class cares about. Now if Moany Drones were talking about bands – Portishead or Massive Attack – that might be different. But all Moany Drones does is drone on about people like Bach and Handel. Dead people. Dead boring people.

Not that I've been listening much. Mostly I've used double music as Dream Time. Dreaming is often the way into a Flash – a Flash of Knowledge, to give it it's proper name. But it's knowledge you know with your heart, not your mind. That's why Dreaming helps. You don't think when you're Dreaming, you just let your mind drift. After that comes a kind of clearing, as if you'd just stumbled through a forest and come to a bright, clear place. And that's when a Flash can happen.

What's funny about all of this is the way teachers are always telling you to think, when actually it's very hard to *stop* thinking. To Dream properly – professionally – you've got to stop your mind altogether and just make a space – a forest clearing – for ideas to flow. It's best to keep your eyes either shut or fixed on one object.

I don't know where the ideas come from. The sky maybe. Or perhaps they're just in the air. Double music is ideal for Dream Practice because Moany Drones makes such a nice soothing sort of drone to go off to. Whenever I find it hard to sleep I try to remember the drone of Moany Drones.

There's always a few wild minutes before he arrives when everyone catches up on the news of the night before. Well, Monika was The

News that morning. There was something about her, some kind of power, that worked like a magnet on the other kids. She was just about mobbed. I began to feel quite angry. I mean whose Minder was she? And from the questions they were all pestering her with, I realized – with a mega-sinking of the heart – that we were meant to start writing up our projects that day.

Monika being surrounded by the others, I was able to ask Jed exactly what we had to do.

"You've got to choose two composers and write about their lives," he said. "At least two pages on each. I'm doing Rachmaninov and Haydn."

"Never heard of them," I said.

"Well, you should have done," said Jed. "Moany Drones has gone on and on about them. He thinks Haydn's the most wonderful thing since sliced bread. Well, before sliced bread really. Haydn was born in 1732. In Austria," he added. Give Jed a few facts and he really likes to show them off.

I could hear the other kids still begging Monika for help.

"Miss! Here, miss! How do you spell Shostakovitch?"

"Miss! Miss! What's sonata form?"

It seemed there was nothing Monika *didn't* know. Also she didn't drone. She had a nice musical sort of voice and she had a funny way

48

of answering questions, like she said,

Shostakovitch,
Got-a-toe-twitch,

and then she spelt it. And "Sonata form," she said, "is rather like two people each with a story to tell. First you hear one story, then the other, and then the two stories come together."

I heard her tell someone else that Schubert wore his specs in bed so he didn't have to waste time putting them on in the morning and could immediately reach for his pen and start writing another tune. I liked the sound of Schubert.

I noticed Lizzie was already sitting down with her notebook open. Not that she was writing in it. She was crying over it. Tears plopped on to her book like invisible ink. I didn't know what to do – pretend I hadn't noticed or ask her what was up? In the end I shoved her an old tissue and moved her book before she drowned it.

Lizzie wiped her eyes, blew her nose and said, "Thanks. Thanks awfully." That's how she talks. I've even heard her call people "darling", or "daahling". I guess she can't help it.

Anyway, I didn't have to ask her what was up, because she told me. "Ma and Pa," she said, "they're splitting."

There was no time for more because Moany Drones came in then. He gave a brief nod to

Monika – as if he'd been expecting her – and she came to sit by me. At least between me and Lizzie. For no reason at all, as far as I could tell, she patted Lizzie's hands. "Pretty hands," she said, "with piano fingers."

When Moany Drones had got us all settled – "Anoraks off, bags in the corner by the door please, and notebooks out." – he said. "Right, everyone. You should all have chosen your composers by now. We'll just go round the class and see who's chosen who."

I wondered if I could risk making up the name of a composer because I couldn't think of a single one. Fortunately Moany Drones started at the other end of the classroom from me. I thought I'd just choose the same names as someone else, only I wouldn't choose the same as Jed. He'd guess. The names were coming fast. Mozart, Bach, Schuman, Vivaldi – I was just trying to memorize a couple when Monika shoved a piece of paper under my nose. Just in time.

"Scully?" said Moany Drones

"Schubert," I said, "and Field."

"Field!" said Moany Drones. "That's an interesting choice."

The rest of the class just found it funny.

"Oh, the famous Green Field," said Tony Riding.

"Brother of Corn Field," said Alison Forster – the class clever clogs.

"Father of Battle Field," said Jed, smirking.

"That'll do," said Moany Drones.

But the whole class had got an attack of the giggles.

"Might I take Scully somewhere quiet," asked Monika with that polite sort of smile I'd seen her use on my parents. The smile that somehow turned a question into a command. "Perhaps help him organize his ideas?"

Ideas? I didn't have a single one.

Moany Drones agreed at once. The giggling turned into a grumbling mutter-mutter-mutter. Finding some reason to escape the classroom is the height of ambition for those in Year 7L.

"Silence!" snapped Moany Drones. "You all have your notes. There's no need for anyone to go to the library. I've brought in all the reference books you might need."

Monika and I tiptoed out while there was a mad rush for the reference books.

"The music room!" Monika ordered. Outside the classroom she suddenly became very excited. She put an arm round me and hurried me along. "Music keeps you safe," she said, and she did a little twirl in the middle of the corridor.

What did she mean, "keeps you safe"? Safe from what? I wondered. But I didn't have time to ask her because now I had to run to keep up with her.

The music room is down in the basement and kept locked because of all the equipment in there – drums, violins, a couple of rather battered cellos. Loads of recorders. Monika must have had this visit planned in advance because she already had the key. In the gloom of the basement I could see she'd taken her boots off. The darkness made her hair glow like the light above a taxi at night.

And then we were in the music room. The blinds were down and I could hardly see anything – just the faint silver shine of the drums. I bumped into the cymbals arranged on a stand and set them shivering. Monika seemed to have vanished. I could just hear her voice.

"Shall I do the blinds?" I asked. "And there must be a light switch somewhere." Somehow I was feeling quite nervous. None of this felt like the "quiet routine" Miss Pugh had suggested. And surely Minders weren't expected to behave strangely? Also, if anything, I now felt more, rather than less alarmed by Monika's "music keeps you safe" remark. I almost thought I could *smell* danger.

"Just a moment!" called Monika, her voice sounding all muffled. The next thing I heard was this music coming from speakers I couldn't even see. It was a sweet, dreamy sort of piano music.

Then Monika flicked up the blinds and I saw her. She wore the swirling blue robe I'd seen in my Flash and she was dancing. Dancing as if she was in some kind of magic trance.

"A nocturne," she said. "Or a night song. John Field, Nocturne Five in B flat major."

I sat on the floor and watched. At first I was just too startled to move – it was all so like the Flash I'd had when she came to our house. The Flash that was the same as Mum's Seeing. Both of us, in our different ways, had seen Monika dancing in a blue robe. Just as she was now. I couldn't swear to it, but I think that after a few minutes, when Monika's dance seemed to circle me and the silk robe flicked my cheek, I think I might have slept. Ever so briefly. When I woke up, just sort of snapping awake, I had the awful thought that Monika's dance was some kind of spell.

That thought made me feel all hot and yet shivery, as if I was about to go down with flu.

Just what sort of a Minder had I got? I wondered. And then I heard myself saying, "Monika, who chose you to be my Minder?"

"Why the Authorities, of course," said Monika.

THE AUTHORITIES

Soon as school was over I decided to go and see Dad down in the market. Lizzie walked part of the way with me. Usually, the BMW's waiting outside for her. It's never her mum or dad inside, usually some slave or other – a secretary or gardener or even her dad's chauffeur. Lizzie goes bright red when it's the chauffeur in his peaked cap.

"No one collecting you today?" I asked.

"I told them I wanted to walk," she said, "and everyone was too stressed out to object. Ma and Pa were screaming at each other and everyone else was trying to keep out of the way. My ma's going on about being penniless and my pa's just knocking back the whisky."

"What, at breakfast?"

"It's what he does when there's trouble," said Lizzie.

"Sounds awful," I said.

"It is," said Lizzie.

"But your mum – I mean your ma – won't really be penniless will she?"

Lizzie shrugged. "It's impossible to tell. One moment they're talking of sending me away to school – for my own good they say – and the next minute my father's ranting about going bankrupt."

"Would you like to go away to school?" I asked.

Lizzie looked all tearful again.

"No," she said. "Would you?"

I thought about it. Some Wizards' kids do go away. There's an Academy in the far north. But they tend to be Class One Wizards (Future Times) who spend their lives up-dating spells and creating new ones and codifying it all. It's all on the Whiznet (that's the Wizards' version of the internet in case you hadn't guessed) and they rarely have contact with People-people. It's a lonely life.

So, "No," I said, "I wouldn't like to go away to school."

"I wish I had a Minder, like you," said Lizzie, all wistful. "It must be great to have someone helping you. Someone you can talk to. And your Ms Brewer looks really nice. Brill hair!"

"She's all right," I said carefully. I badly wanted to tell Lizzie about how strange Monika had been, dancing to that nocturne.

And how I felt I'd been put under a spell.

But I didn't want to say anything yet. Not until I'd spoken to Dad. What was worrying me was the Hat. Dad's Wizard's Hat that had fallen out of the cupboard in the hall when Monika had come to our house. Monika had put it on. Now, that is against all the Rules. In fact it might well be Rule Ten in the Wizards' Commandments – "Thou shalt not let a People-person wear thy magically anointed Hat." Something like that. I don't think I've got the words right, but that's the drift of it. Monika had put it on and gone all dizzy.

Lizzie and I parted at the bus stop – she lives in one of the big Georgian houses up the hill. She waved and smiled as she got on the bus. She's got this really nice smile and blonde hair that's all bouncy and swinging, just like in the telly ads for shampoo.

I walked down to the market thinking about Monika. Once the dancing was over and she was back in her ordinary clothes she seemed OK. We'd sat in the library and she'd told me quite a lot about John Field. He was a poor Irish boy and his father apprenticed him to a man called Clementi. Clementi was a composer too but he also made pianos and he was a very bad Minder. Field never had enough to eat or decent clothes and he had to play the pianos all day long to persuade the customers to buy them.

Perhaps John Field would never have become a composer without his bad Minder. I suppose that's possible. Anyway, when Clementi took the boy on a tour of Russia he ran away and couldn't be found. I think I'd have done the same if I'd been John Field. His life sounded like wall-to-wall homework. Anyway, I easily wrote two pages about him so old Moany Drones should be well pleased. I wouldn't be surprised if I got an A. (Eat your heart out Jed Sullivan.) Monika made me check all my spelling too and be careful with my handwriting. In short she seemed quite normal again except for one thing she said, just as we parted.

"It's very hard being changeable isn't it," Monika said. It was this I was thinking about as I walked down to the market. What had she meant? Did she mean changing from her ordinary clothes into the blue robe? Or did she know? About the Changing Practice? About Wizards?

And then there was "the Authorities". The Authorities who had chosen Monika to be my Minder. I'd been quite satisfied with Monika's answer. At first. She must mean the Local Authorities, I thought. Or the Education Authority. Or the School Governors or ... or... Well, the more I thought about the Authorities, the more doubtful I became. I've heard Dad talk of an almost extinct branch of

Wizards in Finland who are very short of trainees. Rumour has it that they're trying to kidnap a few. Perhaps the Finnish Wizards were The Authorities? Could Monika really be a Wizard-napper? I didn't think so. But something could have happened to her when she put on Dad's Hat. It could have jiggled her brains. Or given her a dose of magic. Anything was possible. And if it wasn't the Hat, then it was something else. Something I didn't know about. Something important that made Monika more than a Minder.

It's quite a walk to the market. You have to go through the big new shopping centre to get to it. I hate this part of town. It makes me feel really hungry for all the things we can't afford – like new trainers and the latest CD – but not quite as hungry as the beggars and buskers in the underpass. And the sellers of *Big Issue*. There was a woman with a baby in the underpass today, playing a recorder really well. I gave her ten pence.

Then the new part of town turns into the old part with narrow cobbled streets and solicitors' offices and a pretty church. Then it's the market.

It was fairly quiet when I got there. Dad had his feet up reading a book. He's been on this one for months. It's called *Conumdra* and it's all in Latin. Dad says it's about Ancient Economics and could be very useful today.

Listening to Dad you'd think there was no such thing as progress. Just one long decline and fall. Everything, according to Dad, was better in the "good old days" and the older the days, the better. Anyway, he wants to visit the university and tell them about the *Conumdra*. He's done this before but I don't think they've ever listened to him. They just think he's an eccentric. Mum says it's one thing to *find* Lost Knowledge but quite another to get it back into circulation.

For once Dad looked really pleased to see me. "Scully!" he said. "How's tricks?"

"Haven't had the chance to practise any," I said.

"Not long till the holidays," said Dad. He always says this even when they're ages away.

"And not long till I meet the Outlandish Gentry," I said.

"I'll do some practice with you tonight," he promised.

"Dad, I'm worried about Monika."

"What's she done? What's she said?" asked Dad getting into his *protective-tiger* mode immediately.

So I told him about Monika dancing in her blue robe in the music room and how odd it had made me feel and how Monika had seemed – well, not herself.

"I'm worried about the Hat," I said.

"The Hat?"

"*Your* Hat. Remember? It fell out of the cupboard and she put it on."

Dad slapped his thighs one after the other and laughed so loudly all the traders turned to look at us.

"That's it! Of course it is!" said Dad. "She's been magicked. Do her a power of good."

"Will it wear off?" I asked.

"Yes. Yes it will. Unless of course it's activated her magic gene."

"Could it do that?"

"It could," said Dad. "Sudden activation of the magic gene can be quite a shock to the system. But we'll have to wait and see. Do you think she'd like her fortune told? That would help us to know what's going on."

"Too risky," I said. I didn't tell Dad about Monika's remark on changing. I hadn't forgotten his idea of making Monika vamoosh. It's just about in his Power. And I had such mixed feelings about her. Part of me really liked her. I felt, like Lizzie, that she was someone you could talk to; someone who was really good at listening. In my opinion there aren't many grown-ups good at that.

"She might learn too much about us," I said.

Dad had just begun to suggest one of his rare spells called the Cloud which he sometimes throws around people when he thinks there's a danger of being discovered, when we were both interrupted by a strange man walking all round the grandfather clock.

Of course you get plenty of odd looking characters in the market. It's one of the things I like about the place. But this old man was particularly strange. For a start he looked very rich and you don't get many rich people coming to the market. He was wearing a grey pin-stripe suit, a huge flowery cravat, a carnation in his button hole and soft grey gloves. And although he was old and frail and walked with a stick, there was something fierce about his face. His nose was sharp, his eyes steely and I noticed that his gold cuff-links were shaped like scorpions.

"Can I help you?" asked Dad.

"A handsome fellow," said the old man, pointing at the grandfather clock with his stick. "Does he sing?"

I could tell Dad liked the question. Clocks are always "he" or "she" to my dad, even clocks that aren't grandfathers or mothers.

"D'you mean does he chime?" Dad asked.

"Yes," said the old man, "that's what I mean. Can I hear him?"

I could tell Dad was rather won over by the way the old man spoke, and by how grand he looked. And of course I suddenly remembered how Dad always said he was "looking after" the clock for someone. Did he know that someone? And was the old man the one? And when Dad said he'd get the pendulum out,

I thought that's what Dad was wondering too.

Dad reached down under the stall and brought out the black velvet glove. The long golden pendulum's a beauty. Dad stroked it once or twice almost as if he were reluctant to hang it inside the clock.

The old man stroked it too with his soft, grey-gloved fingers. I didn't like the way he did it. Greedily and with his eyes all hard and narrow.

"Beautiful," he said. I didn't like the way he said that, either. He said it as if he were looking at a pudding he was just about to gobble up.

Dad opened the door of the clock and hung the pendulum inside. Then using two keys he wound up the clock and moved the hands to five o'clock. The face of the grandfather clock is made of copper and the hands are like a pair of twirly handled, fine-pointed scissors. All round the rim of the clock you can see the phases of the moon. At the base of the clock's door there's a little window so you can see the pendulum gleaming and swinging inside.

All three of us waited for the clock to chime. And when it did everyone in the market fell silent. For as the old man had said, the clock didn't so much chime, as sing. It played a kind of slow deep note three times and then it seemed to reach deep down inside itself to produce five great bongs. I think that clock could out-bong Big Ben any day of the week. Or should I say any hour of the day. The sound was so loud and deep that the body of the clock seemed to shudder with the effort of it.

The old man giggled! A horrid, gleeful, high-pitched giggle. Even Dad seemed bothered by that giggle. "Very impressive!" said the old man when he'd finished giggling. "And what kind of time does it keep, this fellow?"

But Dad had turned cold now. He unhooked the pendulum and slid it back into its velvet case.

"It keeps good time," he said curtly.

"Ah," said the old man. "You'll have tinkered with it a little then. I've known grandfathers like this that keep only bad time. Oh very bad time indeed. Of course Time can't be kept, we all know that. But there's good time and there's bad. We all know that too."

I was about to ask the old man the difference between good time and bad because I had the feeling he didn't just mean accurate or inaccurate time. But Dad seemed very uneasy now. He was back on his stool behind the stall and he'd picked up a watch he was mending.

"Good time or bad," he said, "the clock's not for sale."

"Quite so," said the old man as if not in a million years had he thought it was. "This your boy then?" he asked, nodding at me.

"Yes," said Dad. His face had become quite

snarly now. I could tell he was wishing he'd never begun talking to the old man, and had just been falsely charmed by the old man's age, his grand clothes, his way with words, his interest in the clock's song.

And then the old man asked a very strange question indeed. "And what sort of Time d'you keep," he asked, looking straight at me. And because he'd fixed me with his steely eyes and the sharp question of his nose, I said the first thing that came into my head.

"I keep Present Time, sir," I said.

That seemed to please him. "I'm very glad to hear it," he said. "Perhaps I'll come and hear the grandfather's song again. Some other time."

And then he was gone. I won't say he vamooshed because I don't think he possibly could have done. Just that for an old man he moved very fast.

"Well," I said to Dad, "what d'you think that was all about?"

"I've an idea it was all about you," said Dad. "And I don't like it." And more than that he wouldn't say.

A FLASH AND
A COMMAND

I have to jump a bit here because last night I had this amazing Flash.

I was in a really big sulk because when we got home, Dad and I, everything went wrong. So wrong that in the end I just flopped on my bed in the dark.

There was so much planned for the evening. Dad had promised to help me with my Changing Practice. That was one plan. And I was going to quiz him about the grandfather clock and the old man. That was plan two. All the way back from the market my head had been bursting with questions about Time.

I could hardly believe I hadn't thought – thought properly, that is – about Time before. I mean I've just been in it. I suppose fish are like this about water. It's what they live in and they don't suddenly flap their fins and say "Aha! This is water!" All the old man's talk about good Time and bad Time and the impossibility of "keeping" Time had made me feel strangely *outside* Time. But that's the wrong way of describing it. As I lay on my bed in the darkness, it was more as if the present moment had gathered within itself, *all* Time. Time Past and Time Future, held in a single moment. Perhaps it was this that brought about the Flash. I'm not sure I could do it twice. But I hope so.

Anyway, apart from Changing Practice and quizzing Dad, plan three was to tell Mum about Monika dancing. I thought Mum might be able to See into it. Explain it.

Well none of this happened. Not plan one, two or three. When Dad and I got home the Telepod in Dad's den was bleeping like mad, Mum's washing whirligig was sending out sparks and there was a letter on the mat. A letter with my name on the front – Erasmus (Scully) Browne in purple ink.

I stood in the hall and opened it very carefully. Dad was almost hopping with impatience, desperate to know what was in the letter and desperate to get to his bleeping Telepod. There was a low mumble of voices from the sitting room so I knew Mum had a client.

The letter was very brief. Well, I don't know if you'd call it a letter. It was more of a command. Across the top, in the same purple ink as on the envelope, it said OUTLANDISH

GENTRY in funny decorated letters like the ones monks used to draw and paint when they were copying out the psalms or something. And underneath, in plainer writing, it said:

It is hereby ordained that one
Erasmus (Scully) Browne
shall appear before
THE OUTLANDISH GENTRY
on Monday, midnight, being
the fourth day of the 10th month.

"That's next week!" I said, and I could hear my voice squeaking.

"Scully," said Dad, clasping me by the shoulders, "just hang in there. I'll be back as soon as I can." Then he dashed up the stairs to his den and the Telepod.

"How far back?" I shouted after him. "How far back are you travelling?" I hate not knowing where he's going. It's bad enough not knowing how long he's going to be away. He shouted something but I didn't catch it. The "something-century" was all I heard.

Dad's a bit of a specialist in the sixteenth and seventeenth centuries so I expect it was one of those. Sometimes when he comes back from the sixteenth century he talks like someone in a Shakespeare play and it's fatal to send him shopping or anything. "Vex not the moment," he'll say when Mum fails to pass him the marmalade at breakfast.

I could hear the Telepod clacking out a message on the computer and then Dad shouting at it – probably because he'd pressed the wrong buttons. The Telepod itself is big but simple. It's like a large globe with levers all over it for the different centuries. The BC ones are blue and go in minus tens. And the AD ones are small and yellow and numbered one to twenty-one. When Dad's "on call" (as he puts it) the Telepod lights up and one of the levers flashes. All he has to do (when he's managed the instructions on the computer) is put on his gear and push the handle down. It makes the house shake a bit but Mum and I are used to that.

Dad explained to me once that just as the Earth turns round the Sun, certain moments of Time are caught in the light and give out fresh energy. "People think that the Past is something that's over and done with," said Dad, "but it's not. Every moment of Time is packed with a certain amount of energy. Sometimes a moment is so charged with energy it can take thousands of years before all of it is released."

I don't think I really understood this when Dad first explained it. But I'm beginning to now. I think it means that the Past is always with us, even when we don't know it.

I know Dad's journeys are all very important. I know how upset he gets when he's spent days in another century and has brought nothing back. And how excited he gets when he's found a fragment of an old astronomer's notebook or a few lines of an unknown poem. He spends hours in his den then, recording it all, trying to work out its relevance to today's physics or literature and how he can pass the Knowledge on. I know all that. But I miss him when he's away. Sometimes, because his mind is so stuck in the Past, I feel as if he and I don't live in the same world. Even when he's with his clocks, he's not really in *this* world.

I stood in the hall with the letter in my hand. Very soon there was the shudder in the house and I knew Dad had gone. From the sitting room there was the murmur of voices, soft voices floating off into the Future. They were like the cooing of doves in the tall trees of our park.

That's when I felt it. That strange feeling of each second echoing with Time Past and Time Future. It was almost like being out in space, which is why I went up to my room and lay in the dark with absolutely nothing in my head but this huge space of Time. And then it began.

While it's happening, a Flash is like a long wide-awake dream. It's only afterwards, when it's over, that you feel it's *flashed* past.

It began with my seeing Monika and the old man from the market dancing together. She was in her blue robe and he was in his pin-stripe suit and they were both barefoot. It wasn't a happy dance. It was more like a war dance. There was a lot of stamping. They were both punching the air with their fists. The next thing I saw was myself joining in. I was barefoot too and it was as if I was the object of their war dance. I felt myself spinning between the two of them, as if each had some power drawing me first to one, then to the other until I was dizzy and reeling.

Somewhere in the distance, sitting on a kind of grassy bank, I saw Lizzie. She sat with her knees hunched up to her chest and she was crying.

I think words were spoken. I think I heard drums and cymbals, but I can't be sure of that. What I did know – what the Flash revealed – was that there was some connection between Monika and the strange old man. And that connection was me!

BREAKING THE RULES

The Flash left me exhausted. I just about managed to crawl into my pyjamas. I heard Mum's client leaving and Mum bolting the front door. Then I was asleep. I slept so late there was hardly time for breakfast, let alone my Changing Practice. I felt kind of hot with panic when I thought of the Outlandish Gentry Test now only six days away. For that matter I hadn't yet finished my two pages about Schubert. I'd got an A for my piece on John Field and an astonished comment from Moany Drones. "Awake at last, Scully," he'd written. "Excellent work. Keep it up." But I hadn't. I hadn't even begun on Schubert. Monika was not going to be pleased.

Monika. I wondered how she would be today. In fact I had a quick look at the timetable. No Music. Science, Maths, Spanish and English.

There was no sign of Dad. That meant Mum would take over the clock stall for the day. She likes doing it. Says she gets quite a few new clients that way. She has little cards she hands out saying *Mathilda Browne. Tomorrow's secrets told today. Confidential Service. Astrological Charts extra.* Should I tell Mum about the strange old man, I asked myself? "Unwise", was the answer to that one. Dad worries. Mum panics.

Thinking about the old man gave me what felt like a scary but daring idea. What if I suggested to Monika a visit to the market? That way she and the old man might come together and I might find out what both of them were up to. The old man had said he'd come back – to hear the "song" of the grandfather – but he hadn't said when. Inviting Monika to see Dad's clocks would be a bit of a long shot. And if I *did* manage to bring the two of them together, could I cope? I didn't imagine all three of us would suddenly start dancing. The dance in my Flash meant something else. It had been as if both Monika and the old man had wanted me for something. But what?

I was puzzling about all this as I walked to school. I saw the BMW purring down the road from the opposite direction and I saw Lizzie get out, slamming the door behind her without even a glance at the driver.

Monika was waiting for me outside room

72

thirty-four, looking anxious but OK. Reasonably calm. I felt a sigh of relief go right through all my bones. I really didn't fancy another dancing session. Monika's calmer appearance suggested that Dad's Hat had just done a temporary magicking from which Monika had now recovered.

"Hurry up, Scully," she called when she saw me.

"I haven't finished Schubert," I gabbled, "but I got an A for John Field..." I regretted mentioning Field. I thought he might start Monika dancing again. But Monika seemed to have other things on her mind.

"I'm with you all day today," she said. "I'm a full-time Minder! Have you got your Science book? Did you read up that chapter on the solar system?"

All the time she was asking me questions, Monika was looking over her shoulder as if she was expecting someone to creep up on her. It made me twitchy. Made the hairs on the back of my neck tingle. And the news that Monika was going to be with me *all day* was a bit of a downer too.

I'd decided that with the Outlandish Gentry Test so close, I'd have to break the rules. I'd have to do some of my Changing Practice and Dreaming in school as well as out. It meant I'd have to keep sneaking away – after all there's a limit to the number of times you can ask to go to the lavatory. My only other choice was to work a small Spell on Monika. It's one I've practised on Mum – the Forty Winks Spell – but I've always had Dad there, supervising, just in case I can't bring Mum out of it.

Fortunately I didn't have to try it on Monika because – as now seemed usual – I had to share her with the rest of the class.

We'd been doing the solar system in Science. Half the class were drawing a picture to show where all the planets were in relation to the Sun and the other half were trying to answer the questions set by Mr Gale, the Science teacher.

Mr Gale is good on Science. Trouble is he gets so excited about it that sometimes he can barely speak. Also he's not much good at keeping order. He tries to answer everyone's questions at once and then when there's so much noise he can't hear himself speak, he gets angry and flings his arms about and starts shouting. Once he even flung a book across the room. Just missed Alison Forster.

Anyway, I could tell Mr Gale was very glad to have Monika there. Somehow or other she is a quietening influence. I think it's her voice, all slow ups and downs like the sea on a gentle day. Also it's the way she pulls up a chair beside you and gives you her full attention as if there's no one else in the room but you. Whoever she sits by seems brighter, more alive – as if they get a kind of buzz from that wild ginger hair.

Facing me I could see Jed, head down over the questions and already writing fast. Lizzie was doodling. She looked very pale. I thought again of how I'd seen her in the Flash – sitting on a grassy bank with her knees huddled against her chest, crying. Crying, I thought, because she was left out; because she couldn't help and wanted to. It made me think that I mind about Lizzie and Lizzie minds about me. Perhaps we're both Minders!

I started doing my drawing of the solar system – rather slowly because I wasn't quite sure what to put where and we had to match the distance in space with the distance in centimetres on our graph sheets. I knew that from the Sun outwards, the planets were Mercury, Venus and Earth and I knew that Pluto was the one furthest away. It was the rest I was uncertain about. Anyway, what I was really concentrating on wasn't the planets. It was a spider I'd seen making a web high up in the corner of the classroom, just above Mr Gale's desk.

A preliminary Changing Exercise – an Exercise that's a kind of warm-up to Changing yourself – is Changing something else. So I considered the spider. In fact I had a rush of ambition that almost made me laugh out loud. Could I Change the spider into an elephant or a kangaroo? Imagine it hopping about the classroom! Or maybe one of those wild Arab horses with a silky mane and a plume of a tail. I could leap on its back and with one arm reach down and hoist Lizzie up behind me, then we'd gallop off into some happy-ever-after sunset. I could almost hear the hooves and imagine Lizzie waving to an astonished face gazing through the windscreen of the BMW. Day-dreaming about that almost made me forget the spider.

When I looked at it again it seemed to be doing a neat repair job on its web. Anyway, there are certain Wizard rules about proportions. Making something small into something very large, or something very large into something very small, is considered Poor Practice and of considerable danger to the creature involved.

So I settled on a kitten. I fixed my eyes on the spider and I thought *kitten. Black kitten.* And I watched the spider suddenly go very still and then swell and struggle a little as if shaking itself free of its spider self, and the next moment there was a kitten.

And pandemonium! I suppose the kitten was in a state of shock to begin with. It leapt on to Mr Gale's desk. Then it raced round the tables knocking off pens and pencils, sending rubbers flying, skidding on charts of the solar system. It hit the window-sill as if it was making a dash for the open and didn't yet know about glass. This made it wilder still. (I half suspected that a bit of a wild Arabian horse had got into that kitten. You have to have a very *clear* mind when you're doing the Changes.)

It was useless Mr Gale shouting at everyone and telling them to sit down and shut up. Everyone was dashing around trying to catch the kitten, wondering where it had come from, making *pussy, pussy, pussy* noises. As for me, I felt truly, deeply, badly. It was impossible for me to turn the kitten back into a spider. Not only was there too much noise and excitement to allow me the concentration, but everyone was watching. When I've Changed things before I've been on my own (or with Dad). It's been very quiet. And quick. We turned our dog Slooch into a pig for about five minutes. (I think he quite enjoyed it.) And a tadpole into a goldfish for about two seconds – long enough for it to do a single golden length of the pond. And of course I've Changed apples into oranges and carrots into chips. But that doesn't really count.

What was uppermost in my mind just then was what you might call the First Command-ment of the Wizards' Code. Which is that all creatures must be returned to their Original Form. And there was this poor frantic kitten and no way could I turn it back into a spider.

It was Monika who caught the kitten. She sat very still and quiet, just making soft noises and when – on its umpteenth flight round the classroom – the kitten landed in her lap, she just held on to it, gently but firmly, stroking its head and back and saying, "There. There. You're quite safe." The whole class went absolutely still. It's a wonder the planets themselves didn't stop revolving.

Then, still holding the kitten, Monika rose to her feet.

"Scully!" she said. "Outside!"

I trailed after her. I could hear Mr Gale clapping his hands and saying, "Now quiet everyone. Settle back to work. You've half an hour before the bell."

Monika and I sat in the hall where we all have lunch – well, those of us who don't skip off to the chippy or down to the baker's where they'll warm you up a nice fat slice of pizza or some yummy sausage rolls. Monika still held the kitten in her lap.

"Scully," she said, "that was very dangerous. Now will you please turn this poor kitten back into whatever it was before!"

A SECRET AGENT

So she knew!

I just gawped at her. I expect my mouth had fallen open wide enough to catch a dozen flies and several spiders. Looking at Monika now, her arms full of kitten, her hair like a chrysanthemum in new bloom, I had no doubt at all that she had a fully activated magic gene all of her very own. It didn't need Dad's Hat to set it going. It had been ticking away nicely all by itself for years. Suddenly Monika seemed – well, powerful.

"Scully," she said, while I sat there dumbstruck and she continued stroking the cat, "I'll explain later. Now will you please stop looking so astonished and *do* something for this kitten that doesn't want to be a kitten!"

"Yes," I said. "Yes, I will." Actually I think it was the hardest piece of Changing I've ever had to do. I had to close my eyes first to bring up the calm and the concentration. Then I stared at the kitten and I thought *spider*. I thought *eight hairy legs*. I thought *fat black middle*. I thought *scuttle and spin*. I thought *sticky grey gossamer web*. And then it was done.

Monika gave a little "eech!" as the kitten on her lap ran down her leg as a spider, considered going into her boot, thought better of it and ran happily under the classroom door. I doubt anyone in there noticed.

"That," said Monika, "was very dangerous."

I think I probably blushed. "I know," I said. "And I'm sorry. It's just that I've only got six days left before…" I hesitated. I still didn't really know who Monika was.

"Before your Test by the Outlandish Gentry," Monika said. She was grinning now and looking very pleased with herself. I felt rather cross.

"Look," I said, "I thought you were my Minder."

"I am," she said. "Isn't that obvious yet?"

"I mean my *school* Minder," I said. "Didn't Miss Pugh bring you in? And what about the Authorities?"

"Oh, Miss Pugh," said Monika airily, as if our headmistress was a mere nobody. "She has nothing to do with the Authorities. I tell you what, let's go out into the playground. There's

80

no one there until break and we won't be over-heard."

"Mr Gale...?"

"I'll tell him that too much excitement is bad for you at the moment and that I thought you needed quietening down. Which," she added, as we made our way outside, "is quite true."

Only what happened outside wouldn't quieten anyone. The playground itself was empty. It's a bleak, grey, tarmaced square which only an extremely dull and stupid grown-up could possibly call a *playground*, but looking over the wall and obviously waiting was the old man. The old man from the market.

I'd found him scary in the market, but seeing him at the school gate, still in his immaculate pin-stripe suit, his greedy eyes watching, a scorpion cuff-link glinting at his sleeve – well that was even more scary. And spooky. I could feel a kind of cold shiver run all over me as if my body was giving me a warning. A warning of danger. And Monika confirmed it. Monika grabbed my hand and cried, "Run, Scully! Run!"

Not that she gave me a choice. The shiver had barely reached my toes when she was dragging me round the back of the school and when, looking back, I saw the old man – suddenly surprisingly agile – climb over the wall and start running after us – I didn't need further encouragement.

We doubled back through the school, down the *up* stairs, up the *down*, through the back entrance and out into the street. Soon we were dodging down side-roads until I was completely lost. And out of breath. Monika seemed to have wings on her boots and the old man didn't give up that easily. We only lost him after about the sixth left turn.

"Where are we going?" I puffed.

"My house," Monika shouted.

I ran blindly after her. I was remembering my Flash and how the dance had been like a war dance with Monika and the old man pulling me apart. What if I'd got it all wrong? What if Monika wasn't rescuing me (as it seemed) but really Wiz-napping me for the Finnish Wizards? Or the Icelandic Wizards? Or the Wizards of Timbuktu? And why was all this happening when there were only days to go before my Test by the Outlandish Gentry?

I think it was being lost down all those side-roads that made me panic, because when we reached Monika's house, and after we'd more or less fallen through the front door and Monika had locked and bolted it behind us, I felt better. I felt safe.

Monika's house was nothing like I imagined. Not that I'd given her house much thought, but somehow I'd expected it to be modern and stylish. Stylish with a capital S.

And probably uncomfortable.

So I lay on the floor gasping for breath and gasping with astonishment. It was more like being in a garden than a house. We'd come into what seemed to be a huge conservatory. Around the sides of it, this glass dome, were broad slatted shelves with pots of all shapes and sizes on them and flowers – almost a jungle of flowers – flowers climbing, tumbling, shooting up sticks, budding and blossoming. It was October outside, but in here it was still summer.

I must have been gawping again, because Monika started to laugh. There she was, sitting on the door-mat, boots stuck up in front of her, laughing her ginger head off.

"I don't see what's so funny," I said. "I don't think I've ever had such an awful morning."

"Your face!" said Monika pointing a finger at me. "You look like someone who's stepped off the planet."

I had to grin back at her. "This place," I said, "all these flowers…"

"I grow things," said Monika. "Minding. Growing. They're much the same." She got up from the mat and dusted herself down. Little bristly door-mat hairs clung to her miniskirt. "Come on. Let's have a cup of tea. And I've a chocolate cake. I think we need something comforting, don't you?"

"What d'you mean," I asked, following her to the kitchen, "about Minding and Growing being much the same?"

"Well," said Monika, putting the kettle on, (it was a very stylish lime-green kettle) "if you Mind something that's alive you help it to Grow, don't you?"

"I suppose you do," I said. I found myself thinking of Lizzie and how no one seemed to be helping her to Grow.

There weren't quite so many flowers in the kitchen, but there was still a fair number. Bunches of dried herbs hung from a pole. Winter pansies were beginning in a window-box and on the table there was a bowl of hyacinths, still folded into themselves so you could just see the beginnings of blue. A vast cheese plant (something like Jack's beanstalk, I thought) was heading for the ceiling, and out-side, through the kitchen window, I could see a great barrel of late nasturtiums as bright and gingery as Monika's hair. In fact she might well have washed her hair in them.

If Monika was as good at Minding as she was at Growing, then she was very good indeed. I felt a whole lot better sitting down at her kitchen table – particularly when there was a chocolate cake on it and two mugs of tea. Monika didn't seem to care when I stirred two teaspoons of sugar into mine. (Mum always tuts and says, "Your teeth, Scully!")

I had to eat the cake quickly because I was bursting with questions I couldn't ask with my mouth full. As if she'd guessed this, Monika said, "Ask. Ask whatever you like and I'll try and answer."

"How do you know about the Changing Practice? How do you know about the Outlandish Gentry? Who's the old man? D'you know he came to the market? What does he want and…"

Monika held up her hand. "One question at a time would be easier," she said. "I'll try to begin at the beginning. When Miss Pugh said you were going to have a Minder, she told you the truth. But not all of it."

"What did she leave out?"

"She left out that I was an Agent."

"You mean like a double agent? A spy?"

Monika laughed. "No. I'm an Agent for the Outlandish Gentry. They have to have outworkers to protect the trainees. There are quite a lot of us – Agents, I mean – dotted all over the country."

"But why do we need protecting?" I asked.

"That's more difficult to explain," said Monika pouring herself a second mug of tea. "You see, at the age when a Wizard is coming into his Powers, he's very vulnerable—"

"Vulnerable?"

Monika looked at the bowl of hyacinths on the table. "Like that," she said.

"You mean someone could stop them flowering," I said.

"That's exactly what I mean," said Monika. "Or worse," she added. Her face had turned very grave.

"Worse? What do you mean 'worse'?" I asked. I could feel my legs beginning to tremble under the table.

"There are those entirely against magic," said Monika. "Those who would like to banish it from the world or use it for their own purposes."

"But why? And for *what* purposes?" I asked.

"You can control people's thoughts." said Monika.

"You mean like the ads on the box?" I said.

"Oh much more than that," said Monika. "Think schools. Think parents. Think newspapers. Books. Politicians. How many of your thoughts do you think belong to you? Are your own original ones?"

"I don't know," I said. "I haven't thought about my thoughts!"

"There you are then," said Monika. "Magic is your own and no one else can control it. That's why it's dangerous. And that's why it's important that no one neglects their magic gene."

"But the people who want to banish magic," I said, "and use it for their own purposes. Who are they? And what do they want?"

"They're mostly in disguise," said Monika. "The Outlandish Gentry are trying to find out more about them. Particularly since..." She hesitated. I knew immediately there was something nasty that she didn't want to tell me.

"Particularly since..." I prompted.

"There was a trainee," said Monika reluctantly, "caught and sieved—"

"Sieved?" I couldn't believe my ears. I couldn't even take another bite of chocolate cake. Mum has a sieve. She uses it to drain the water from a pan of vegetables or pasta. How could you *sieve* a person?

"We believe it's like a blood test," said Monika miserably. "You know, like they use a syringe to take a sample of blood out of you?"

"They drain out the magic..." I said. I'd gone horribly cold even though it was warm in Monika's kitchen. And I felt all tightly folded up inside, as tightly folded as the hyacinths.

"How was he afterwards?" I asked in a very small voice. "The trainee they sieved?"

"Oh, well enough," said Monika. "But you could see it in his eyes."

"See *what*?" I almost shouted. I felt as if I was dragging things out of Monika like you drag your legs out of very tight jeans. I was pulling and tugging.

87

"They lost their colour," said Monika after a long silence. "His eyes, I mean. They lost their colour and went sort of dead. No sense of wonder. No magic left. And he's no memory of what happened."

"And what did they do with it, the sieved magic?" I tried to imagine what sieved magic might look like. What colour would it be? Would it look like blood? Would it be a pale, mystical blue? Would it be more like the sap of trees, a sort of gluey white stuff? And how did they keep it? In bottles in the fridge? In test tubes? It didn't bear thinking about.

"It's believed that there's a laboratory somewhere," said Monika, "where they use it in experiments."

"And the old man," I asked, "is he a part of all this?"

"We think he is," said Monika. "Appearing in the market like that was very risky. He must be quite desperate. You see once you're through your OG Test, he can't touch you. So there's not much time left."

"But why was the market risky?" I asked.

"Because of the clock, of course," said Monika. "You *must* know about the clock…?"

THE DROP OF ETERNITY

We didn't get back to school until lunchtime. There was no sign of the old man.

"I might have scared him off," said Monika, looking rather proud of herself. "For the time being," she added.

There were loud calls of "Skiver!" when I went into the lunch hall. Not that I was very hungry after all the frights of the morning, not to mention the chocolate cake. I sat between Jed and Lizzie. Jed was already on pudding while Lizzie was still picking at her veggie burger. In a way, I thought, Lizzie had been *sieved*. The brightness she usually had, had been drained out of her. Yes, *sieved* put it more precisely. It had been slowly drained away. And what could bring it back again, I didn't know.

"What about coming round for tea today?" I asked her. "If you're allowed."

She gave me a small smile – not like the big grin she used to have, but better than nothing. "I'll come," she said, "whether I'm allowed or not."

I can't say my concentration was much good that afternoon. English passed me in a blur. I was too busy thinking of what Monika had told me about the clock. How it was on loan from the Outlandish Gentry and how Dad was its guardian – its Minder, if you like.

"Inside the clock is the Drop of Eternity," Monika said. It set my head reeling, that one. I remembered how Dad used to pat the clock and say "good drop of Eternity in that clock" and how I'd always thought he was joking.

"The Drop of Eternity contains the primary cell of the magic gene," Monika explained. "It's very powerful. It can create new genes. Mixed with sieved magic, there's no knowing what it could do. Perhaps even Eternal Youth."

"But why's my Dad looking after it?" I asked. (And causing me all this aggro, I was thinking.)

"Mainly because if anything should happen to you."

"Like my magic being sieved," I said bitterly.

"Exactly. Well a drop of the Drop of Eternity could save you. Renew the gene. Your father's instructions were to look after the clock until a member of the Gentry came to collect it. That was likely to be just before your Test."

"So Dad could have thought the old man belonged to the Gentry," I said. "Surely he'd recognize another Wizard?"

"Not necessarily," said Monika. "There are certain code words. But we think They might have broken the code."

"They?"

"They call themselves the Scorpions," said Monika. That reminded me of the old man's scorpion cuff-links and made me shiver again. "But we've begun to call them the Pin-stripes because a pin-stripe suit seems to be their usual disguise."

"It's a pity my dad didn't know that," I said.

"Yes," said Monika. "It was a mistake not to inform him."

"So," I said – for it was all coming together in very nasty detail now – "the Pin-stripes, as you call them, are after me *and* the clock."

"Afraid so," said Monika. "My guess is that the old man was just checking that he had the right clock and the right boy. No other clock has a chime like that grandfather clock."

"So now he knows," I said.

"Now he knows," agreed Monika.

"Where's the Drop of Eternity kept?" I asked.

"In the pendulum, of course," said Monika, "held in a small glass phial. If you know how, you can slip the base off the pendulum and there it is. It's probable that the old man will try for the clock first."

"Big deal!" I said. "Me second."

"Cheer up," said Monika, "we believe we're one step ahead of the Pin-stripes. The old man knows he's been recognized. That's sure to make things more difficult for him. And once you're through your Test, your magic's sealed. You're safe."

I must say I didn't feel cheered. Not one tiny bit. And during the last lesson of the afternoon – Spanish – I suddenly had, not a Flash but a terrible thought: Mum. Mum in the market with the clock. And the old man on the prowl. What if he persuaded her to give him the clock? Pretended that Dad had agreed to it, and he'd come to collect? Despite all her Seeing powers, Mum is awfully trusting. Particularly of polite, well-dressed old men.

When the bell rang for the end of school I didn't pause to say bye, see you or cheers to anyone. And I completely forgot about inviting Lizzie to tea. I just fled to the market.

It was only as I was dashing through the underpass that I realized there was one question I'd forgotten to ask Monika: why, in the school music room, had she danced round me like that?

AN ARMY OF CLOCKS

I never got to the market. It happened in the underpass. There's always a crowd down there – shoppers, people going home from work, newspaper and flower sellers, the alcoholics all squatting in a corner with their bottles of cider. And the sales were on so it was busier than ever. People think that lonely dark places are scary, but after this, I think I'll feel more scared of daylight and big crowds.

The crowds made it easy for the Pin-stripe gang. It's all very well for the newspapers to go on about gangs of kids stealing cars – no one talks of gangs of respectable looking middle-aged business men stealing young Wizards. But that's what happened. Those expensive suits were a wonderful disguise. The men looked so wealthy, healthy and important that anyone seeing a couple of them carrying me off would never have suspected a thing. I don't suppose anyone noticed the gold scorpion cuff-links they all wore. If anyone did notice, they probably just thought it was some new fashion. I think I heard one of the men say to an inquiring woman, "Poor boy. He's fainted."

One of the Pin-stripes must have tripped me up. I didn't recognize *my* old man among them, but then I didn't have much chance to recognize anyone before the chloroform gag was on my mouth.

When I came to I was in some enormous mansion out in the country. I knew it was the country because it was so quiet I could hear birds instead of car alarms and sheep instead of ambulance sirens. There were barred wooden shutters over the windows. The ceiling above me looked miles away, but in my woozy state I could see that there was a huge plaster rose in the centre and all sorts of swirling patterns round the edges.

I was lying in a big soft bed in brand new pyjamas and I felt decidedly odd. My own clothes, I saw, were in a pile on a chair. When I tried to get out of bed I felt wobbly and shaky. I could see a mirror over in the far corner and I badly wanted to look in it – to see if my eyes had gone dead, like Monika had said happened to that other trainee Wizard.

I managed to take off my pyjama jacket and examine my arm for holes – some place they might have stuck a needle and sieved the magic out of me. I couldn't see a mark. I shook my head a little because it felt as if it was full of cotton wool and then I lay still, trying to gather my strength to get out of bed.

The house seemed very still. Had the Pin-stripes dumped me here? I thought it unlikely. If they wanted to dump me, it would have been at the side of the road or in a car-park – not in this plush bed in new pyjamas. But the alternative to being dumped was even more scary. It meant that they hadn't done with me yet! How long did it take to sieve someone's magic out? Did they do it all in one go or bit by bit? Sometimes my mum gives blood at the blood transfusion centre. I know they're only allowed to take a pint at a time. Was it like that with magic?

It's amazing what you can do when you're desperate. I swung my legs out of the bed and sat there for a moment until I stopped feeling dizzy. I needed more light before I could check out my eyes in the mirror, so I walked over to the windows. The bar across the shutters was iron and heavy and the shutters looked so old I knew they'd creak. I heaved the bar up and began opening the shutters carefully, stopping and listening at every creak. Nobody came and very soon the room was flooded with light. So much light that it hurt my eyes and I had to sit down on the edge of the bed again. I could see outside now and there was nothing but field after field after field with a ridge of trees in the far distance.

The mirror was one of those full-length ones on a stand so that you can swing it. Probably an antique to judge by the rest of the room. I remembered what Monika had said about the other boy's eyes. Not just that they went dead, but that they'd lost their colour.

My eyes are green. And, when I made it to the mirror, they were still green! I must have stared into that mirror for about five minutes, shutting my eyes and opening them again just to make absolutely sure.

So the next thing I did was to put on all my clothes – except my shoes – and to start thinking about escape. I tried the windows first, but they were all firmly nailed shut. I wondered if I could break one, but looking about me, I saw nothing I could use. And anyway, I was scared of making a noise. Apart from that, the fields outside offered nowhere to hide and I didn't feel quite up to running for the trees on the ridge. I judged them to be at least ten kilometres away.

It never occurred to me that the door would be open. I tried it listlessly. When the handle turned I couldn't believe my luck. But what was outside made me think my head had gone decidedly funny and that I was seeing things.

Beyond my room was a big marble-tiled

hall. And it was crowded with clocks. An army of clocks. Grandfathers. Grandfather clocks of all shapes, sizes and ages. Some with small, plain faces, some with large flowery faces; squat clocks, tall clocks, clocks in beautifully polished cases; dull, neglected clocks; clocks decorated in gold. And they all stood there silently, not a tick out of any of them. In that great grand hall it was as if Time had stopped and they were waiting for me to start it. Perhaps it was because I was still rather woozy that their faces seemed to be pleading with me, as if they were real human grandfathers, saying "Save us! Save us!"

It was obvious from this gathering of clocks that the Pin-stripes had been searching for *our* grandfather, the clock with the precious Drop of Eternity in it. Had they found it? Had Mum handed it over? I looked wildly round me. There was just one clock under a dust sheet. I tiptoed across and lifted the sheet. My heart sank when I recognized its familiar face. It was almost like having my dad there, seeing it. It brought the tears to my eyes. I could have hugged it. I turned the small gold key and opened the clock's door. And I had to stop myself crying out. For the pendulum had gone.

If, as I thought, the old man had persuaded Mum that he'd come to collect the clock, he wouldn't have taken it without the pendulum. That meant that at this very moment the

Pin-stripes could be in their laboratory removing the glass phial that held the Drop of Eternity from inside the pendulum. And if they had that *and* me then it was all over. Either somehow or other I could try and get the phial back or I could try to escape. I didn't think I had much hope of either.

At the front of the hall was a huge oak door, but I could tell, even without trying the great black bolts across the top and bottom of it, that it was well and truly locked. There were so many corridors, I had no idea which one to try. But off the hall was a broad sweeping staircase with stone steps and a polished wooden banister. As I stood there, among the silent clocks, I could hear the distant murmur of voices.

I crept up the stairs. The voices were coming from a room at the front of the house. I looked about me. I needed somewhere to hide in case one of the Pin-stripes should suddenly come out. There was a big chest standing against the wall. I didn't fancy getting into it, but if I had to, I would. I raised the lid so I could get in fast if necessary, then put my ear to the door where the voices came from.

They weren't very distinct, but what I heard was enough to turn me cold with fright.

The first voice I heard was angry. "We've got the boy, but what use is he without the Drop of Eternity?"

"Well, at least we have the right clock now."

"And an empty pendulum," said the angry voice.

An empty pendulum, I was thinking. An EMPTY pendulum! I wanted to cheer!

"Plus," continued the angry voice, "about five hundred useless clocks cluttering my hall." (So it hadn't just been the old man searching for the clock. They'd all been looking for it. Buying up every clock that looked possible.)

"How are we going to get rid of them without causing suspicion?" continued the angry voice.

"Burn them?"

"And lose thousands of pounds? Have you any idea how much this venture has cost me so far?"

There was a lot of sympathetic "ums" and "ahs" at this point, but then a louder voice said, "But we *shall* get the D of E – then think of the reward when we've sieved the boy's magic and mixed it with a drop of the Drop. The demand will go through the roof!"

"I sincerely hope you're right this time. Sieving that child from the North Western Branch proved pretty useless."

"We hadn't got the formula right then," someone protested. "We've done mock-ups of the D of E in the labs. Put together with the sieved serum, we're certain that will do it."

I could hardly believe the way they were talking. D of E and sieved serum, as if it was all an algebraic equation and a human being wasn't involved. And what did the Drop of Eternity and *my* sieved magic equal?

"Eternal Youth," continued the voice, as if in answer to my question, "and an endless supply of new genes. All at a price of course!"

There was a lot of laughter at this. And then someone banged on the table with something and there was silence. "Our problem now," said the first voice, "is how to keep the boy until we've got the D of E. We know – to our cost – that once sieved, the serum can't be frozen. It has to be fresh. The whole idea was that the sieving should be done quickly. *In situ* if possible. With the boy briefly stunned and then left. Now not only will the boy's wretched parents be seeking him but we'll have the Outlandish Gentry on our backs. The father's sure to report this to them. How long will the boy sleep?"

"Another five or six hours," came the reply. I couldn't be sure, but the voice sounded like that of the old man in the market. I pulled a face at the door and stuck my tongue out at it for good measure. Well, if they thought I'd be asleep for five or six hours then I knew I had five or six hours in which to escape. And I knew too that I'd have to use my magic powers to do it. But the next thing I heard really chilled me.

"It's a good job we've got the woman too," said a voice. "That Agent."

"Yes, that dance of hers in the school music room … that nearly wrecked our chances."

"Does the boy know the meaning of the dance?"

"He's unaware that it's a Protection Spell. Of course we'll have to break it before we can extract the magic."

"Can we do that?"

"Shouldn't be a problem."

"Where have you put the woman?"

"In the Keep. We'll use her for the ransom note. The boy in exchange for the D of E. She'll have to be hypnotized into it, of course. But there's no problem with that either."

"Well, gentlemen, I think that's it for now. Everard, keep an eye on the boy. Make sure he stays doped until we've got the Drop and then have everything ready. Remember we can't risk him trying out any magic tricks – however inexperienced he is."

I heard the scraping of chairs then and people moving about. I fled down the stairs, back to the room. I had to fling off my clothes, scramble into the pyjamas and get back into bed.

When Everard – whoever he was – came in, I pretended to be out for the count. He lifted my arm and I just let it flop. Then – very cunningly, I thought – he tickled my feet. Now my feet are probably the most ticklish feet of anyone in the country. But it's amazing what you can do in a life-and-death situation. I just gritted my teeth and kept very still. I didn't even *twitch*.

But when he'd gone I sat up and rubbed my tickled feet really hard while wondering what on earth to do next. It was difficult enough trying to plan my own escape, but now there was Monika to think about. Monika held somewhere called the Keep and about to be hypnotized and sent off with a ransom note. I couldn't just abandon my Minder, could I?

THE PIN-STRIPES

But where was the Keep? I'd visited a castle in Wales once, on a school trip. The Keep had been a narrow tower where prisoners were held. I didn't think this house, big as it seemed, had a tower. All the same, somewhere there must be a room where the Pin-stripes kept prisoners and I'd have to find it.

What I needed, seriously needed, not like when I'd just been practising, was a Flash. A Flash that would give me an insight not only to where Monika was, but *how* she was. Was I calm enough? Could I concentrate? I pulled up my pyjama trousers, made sure all the buttons on the jacket were fastened – it helps to prepare yourself for the Flash – and then I sat cross-legged on the floor and closed my eyes.

I pictured Monika. It struck me that I was *minding* her in my mind's eye. I concentrated first on her wild ginger hair. Then I pictured her brown eyes, her smile, those nifty boots and neat miniskirts. It's amazing what you can and can't remember about a person. What were her hands like, for instance? I had to picture her turning the pages of my reports before I could see them. (They were stubby and she wore a gold ring on her little finger and that day when she'd danced in the school music room, they'd fluttered like small birds.)

And slowly another picture began to grow. Dimly at first, so that it was like a room at dusk and I could just see a figure moving about and the vague shapes of furniture. It was hard to keep still and quiet then, but I did and slowly the room grew lighter and clearer until I saw Monika pacing up and down like a caged tiger. A tired tiger. I made myself study the room carefully. The door was bolted. Presumably the Pin-stripes hadn't bolted mine because they'd drugged me. The window of Monika's room had an entirely different view. I could see some large wheelie bins and an enormous log stack. It must be the back of the house and it must be on the ground floor.

Being inside a Flash is quite exhausting. I wanted to stop there and open my eyes but I forced myself to carry on. I made myself move outside. It was impossible for me to see the back of the whole house. All I could see was a large bulk of light stone. It was like being very short-sighted and looking at a house without your specs. It was all blurred and unfocused. But I could see the wheelie bins and the logs. And I could work out now that to find the room where the Pin-stripes had kept Monika I had to go down a corridor until I got to the back of the house.

I opened my eyes and took several deep breaths. It was one thing to know where Monika was, quite another to get her out – to get us *both* out. I realized with a sinking heart that I'd have to put my Powers to the test. Not the Outlandish Gentry sort of Test, but a real-life test. It was like being asked to give a concert at the Albert Hall without a proper rehearsal, without backing musicians, without a manager, without any help at all.

I opened my door as carefully and quietly as I could. It was beginning to get dark but there wasn't a Pin-stripe in sight. Before, I'd been so astonished by the clocks that I hadn't noticed the narrow, gloomy corridor that ran towards the back of the house. I hurried down it. I seemed to be in the kitchen quarters. I could see the kitchen itself to the left, an enormous dimly lit room with an Aga and a great iron bar above it on which hung huge pans. I had a glimpse of several large baskets full of potatoes and cabbages and carrots. How many Pin-stripes were there that required such huge pans and so many kilos of potatoes?

There was nobody in the kitchen. Perhaps

the cooks had gone off duty until supper time. I hurried past, along another corridor with several doors – each of which could be Monika's Keep. But I didn't have to try them all because from the third one I heard a voice.

Of course, for all I knew the Pin-stripes could have half-a-dozen prisoners. Perhaps there were other trainee Wizards, Wizards already sieved ... but I didn't think so.

"Oh, the brave old Duke of York,

He had ten thousand men;

He marched them up to the top of the hill,

And he marched them down again," sang the voice. Only it didn't sound very brave. There were hiccups in the middle of the marching.

"Monika?" I whispered.

"And when they were up they were up ... Scully? Is that you?" asked Monika. "Are you all right? Have they ... have they ... you know...?"

"Sieved me? No. They think I'm still asleep."

"Thank God for that," Monika whispered. "Scully, never mind me, get away as fast as you can."

"I'm not leaving you here," I whispered back.

"There are Pin-stripe guards back and front," said Monika. "I saw them when they brought me in. But I think you might make it through a side window. Once you're out you'll have to run like the wind."

"I'm not leaving you," I repeated. "Would you mind if I Changed you?"

"Changed me?" said Monika, her voice rising into a squeak. "Into what?"

"An ant," I said. "I've done ants once. You could run out under the door then. I'll do us both."

There was a silence from the other side of the door, then more pacing up and down. I could tell Monika really didn't fancy being an ant.

"I think it's the only way," I pressed. "The Pin-stripes are planning to hypnotize you and send you with a ransom note to Mum and Dad. The Drop of Eternity in exchange for me. Only it will be me sieved of magic."

"It could be the end of Wizardry," said Monika. I could almost hear her hair crackle with anger as she said this. "All right then," she said at last, "I suppose an ant's life isn't that bad. But I'd like to feel confident that you can Change us back again, Scully."

"'Course I can," I bluffed. One thing I did know about Changing someone else is that you have to have their total confidence.

"There's something I've got to do first," I said, "to distract the guards and give us a chance to make a getaway. I'll be back soon. Try and prepare yourself for being an ant."

"I'll try," said Monika in a voice that was almost as small as an ant's – if an ant ever had a voice, that is.

I tiptoed back to the hall of clocks. In the growing darkness the clocks looked almost ghostly. I have to admit I had two motives and one of them was revenge. I wanted to get all those clocks chiming. I wanted to scare those Pin-stripes silly. I wanted to show them they couldn't control Time and they couldn't control magic.

My other motive was more practical. Changing into ants would get us out of the house, but it wouldn't get us far. As ants, it could take us years to get home. But Changed back into ourselves (hopefully) we'd be out in the open. The darkness might hide us, but we'd be lost in it. As far as I could see there was nothing but field and moor beyond the house.

I know all about winding up clocks from Dad. Grandfather clocks have two keys and there's often a mechanism you can switch off or on for the chime. It took what felt like for ever working my way round the clocks. On some of them the noise of the winding sounded as loud as a chain-saw. I set them all to chime at twelve. It wasn't easy. I had to start at quarter to twelve so that by the time I got to the last clock there was just five minutes to go. Then I ran back to Monika's room.

"Are you ready?" I whispered.

"As I'm ever likely to be," said Monika.

"It would help if you could think *ant*."

"I can't!" cried Monika. "I've got cold feet. How many feet has an ant got?"

"Listen!" I hissed at her. "It's our only chance. I've set the clocks going. They're going to chime any minute now. That'll be our chance. The guards will come rushing in and we'll scuttle out – six legs each, OK. We'll be back into ourselves and out of sight before they come looking for us."

"All right," said Monika. "I'm thinking *ant*."

As Monika spoke the clocks began to chime. They chimed and bonged and tolled and sang and rang like they were announcing the finest day in the world. And somehow they sounded so magnificent that I thought *now, now is the moment when I really come into my magic Powers*, and I shut my eyes tight and I whispered the secret words of the Changing Spell and even through the door I could feel Monika shrinking and shrinking and I knew she was nearly there, was nearly ant. The clocks still chimed and rang and I heard Monika whisper, "I'm going, Scully! I'm going!"

I knew then it was time to switch the force from Monika to myself. I knelt on the floor, so as to be ready. I was about to begin on the legs when suddenly someone was shining a blinding light in my eyes and there were two Pin-stripes behind me, one of them forcing my arms behind my back, and the other shouting "Get-up.Get-up.Get-up!"

I was marched back up the corridor, but not before I'd seen Monika – well, not Monika exactly – crawling under the door. *As a woodlouse.*

RESCUE

I had to stop myself shrieking "Monika!" after the departing woodlouse. I couldn't imagine how the spell had gone wrong and I have to admit that as the guards dragged me back up to the corridor, I felt complete despair.

That was surely the end of Monika, I thought. I'd been trying to Mind her and instead I'd turned her into a woodlouse and even if I could ever find her again, I doubted I'd be able to turn her back into Monika again. The best I could do was to wish her a happy woodlouse life.

I felt so bad about Monika it almost distracted me from my own danger. But not for long. I couldn't see the guards until they thrust me back on to the bed, but then I saw that one of them was the old man. He was wearing a white coat over his suit. I could see the scorpion cuff-links glinting under the sleeves. His eyes were like chips of ice.

"You tricked us," I said, I was so angry. "Pretending to be a nice old man. Getting my dad to set the clock going for you."

"Your mum tricked us," he snarled back. "It was she who took the Drop of Eternity out of the pendulum. Oh, a very sharp cookie, your mum."

I could feel a broad grin spreading over my face. Good old Mum! She'd handed over the clock, but first she'd removed the phial containing the Drop of Eternity from the pendulum. But the grin didn't last long.

"Your mum and your Minder – caused us no end of extra trouble, those two," said the old man. "Now we're going to have to indulge in a little robbery, aren't we? The Scorpion Squad are at this very moment making their way to your happy home." And with that he pushed his face so close to mine that his nose was like a beak about to peck out my eyes.

He reached into his pocket and brought out a syringe. "We, the Scorpions," (he spoke the name proudly) "think of ourselves as bankers. We just want to bank the magic. Your magic. You could call us Minders – of a sort!"

Then the needle was in my arm. The last I heard was the old man's horrible evil giggle. And my last thought was *Poor Monika. Monika woodlouse.* Then I was out for the count. Again.

When I came round it was pitch black outside and I was lying in a room that looked like a hospital theatre, strapped down on some kind of sheeted trolley. There were a number of masked, white-coated men around me but I could just about see, under the white coats, Pin-striped trousers.

Most terrifying of all was that above me was a fine wire net. It was like what you might imagine the inside of an electric blanket to be, and there were electrical leads running from each corner, attached to a machine with a variety of dials and levers. I was in no doubt what it was. The Sieve!

I tried to move but found my wrists and ankles had been firmly bound. The only thing I seemed able to move was my head and I almost wished I couldn't because when I turned it I saw one of the Pin-stripes advancing towards me with an even larger syringe than the old man had used. There was purple liquid inside it. The Scorpion Squad, I thought. They'd got the Drop of Eternity so now they could sieve me. And if they had the Drop of Eternity it meant they probably had my mum and dad too. It felt like the end of everything. I almost thought I'd be glad of the needle, the Sieve, the end of magic. Probably if I lived through this I wouldn't be able to feel anything any more. And I'd be glad. I wouldn't even care if my eyes turned grey.

But just as I was thinking all this, the Pin-stripe with the syringe fell back with a kind of "Aagh!" of horror, and soon all the others were pushing off their masks and rushing for the door.

Then I saw them. A whole army of them. Woodlice! They simply swarmed and crawled everywhere, very slowly, as woodlice do. But they seemed to be lined up in legions and there was no end of them. Even as I twisted my head, I could see more of them trundling under the door like miniature tanks. A couple of legions mounted the trolley and climbed all over me. One of them, I knew, was Monika, but which one I hadn't the slightest idea.

I could hear shrieks and yells coming from all parts of the house. Monika must have marshalled all the woodlice of the country. I started to laugh. I suppose I was slightly hysterical because even though the woodlice had scared off the Pin-stripes and stopped the sieving process, there was no way they could untie me.

I was still laughing when I heard a crunch of wheels on the gravel path and the sound of a car that was somehow very familiar to me. I was so befuddled that it took me several min-utes to recognize the BMW, Lizzie's BMW, and by then Lizzie herself, Lizzie's dad, my dad and mum were all in the room; and Mum was crying over me and Dad was untying me and Lizzie was brushing off the woodlice and all I could think of to say was, "Don't stand on them! One of them's Monika!"

Actually the woodlice seemed very adept at avoiding feet and anyway most of them were crawling over the Pin-stripes.

Believe it or not, Mum had brought a flask of tea with her and I wasn't allowed to ask a single question until I'd drunk two mugfuls. Even then, Dad said, "Questions later, son. We've got to get the Drop of Eternity back and we've got to make sure none of this equipment will ever work again." And saying that he ripped all the leads from the machine attached to the Sieve, spoke a few words to it I'd never heard in my life before, and the thing fizzled and sparked and went dead.

"But how did you find me? And Lizzie. Why are you here – and your dad?" I couldn't stop myself asking.

"I'll explain later," said Lizzie grinning. I must say she was looking her old self again, all bright and pretty. Very pretty.

"We don't want them to escape with the phial," said my mum.

"But Monika..." I said. "I can't leave Monika as a woodlouse."

"We won't," said my father. "That's going to be one Changing Spell that you really get right," and he ruffled my hair.

We didn't have to worry about the Pin-stripes escaping with the phial containing the Drop of Eternity. They were being looked after – Minded, you could say – by the woodlice!

The Pin-stripes were all in the hall with the clocks, and the woodlice were swarming all over them, particularly their faces and eyes. And as fast as they brushed away one legion, another followed. I hoped Monika wasn't one of the ones dashed on to the floor. I'd thought woodlice were rather dull before, now I thought them the bravest creatures in the world.

It was Lizzie's dad who dealt with the Pin-stripes.

"Rope," he said. "I've plenty of rope in the boot. I've just used some of it to tie up the guards." And out he went to the BMW and came back with a great coil of rope. He and Dad tied all the Pin-stripes together, in a kind of bundle, like you might firewood. They were still wriggling to try and free themselves from the woodlice.

"Just a minute," said Mum. She'd gone off into one of her trance-like states. "The phial," she said. "I can See it. It's in his pocket." And she pointed at the old man.

Dad reached into the pocket of the old man's white coat and eased out the phial. "Present, Past and Future," he said, holding it up to the light, "all in one," and he handed it to Mum.

When all the Pin-stripes were tied up, Dad stood in the centre of the hall among the still ticking clocks and said, "I'm afraid I shall simply have to do a vamooshing Spell."

"Not the Pin-stripes," I said, because although I thought they deserved vamooshing, they *were* human beings ... of a sort.

"No, silly," said Dad. "The Outlandish Gentry will be here soon. *They* can deal with the Pin-stripes. I meant the woodlice. I'll just vamoosh them to where they came from."

"But you can't," I protested. "You'll vamoosh Monika too."

"Monika is only a temporary woodlouse," said Dad. "She won't be affected by this Spell."

"Are you sure?"

"Scully, may I remind you that you are still a trainee," said Dad, "and that I have conducted more Spells than you have had hot dinners and that furthermore I have been forced to make a special journey back from the twelfth century just to rescue you."

"Yes, Dad," I said.

"Right then," said Dad. "Everyone stand back."

A LATIN SPELL

Of course Dad had to make a big performance out of his vamooshing Spell. Lizzie's dad was sent to fetch his Wizard's Cloak and Hat from the BMW. The Pin-stripes, all bundled together, began to tremble with fright when Dad swirled the cloak like a matador about to attack a bull. Obviously they thought Dad was about to vamoosh *them*. And equally obviously Dad was going to *let* them think that. He spent some time twirling his moustache, settling his Hat on his head, even taking out a comb and combing the few wisps of hair that peeped out from under the Hat.

Once he'd got his gear on, he stretched out his arms like the conductor of an orchestra does before the music begins. (It was a bit as if the woodlice were his orchestra.) Lizzie was looking almost as anxious as the Pin-stripes.

"Mr Browne! Mr Browne! You're not going

to kill the woodlice are you?" (Lizzie is very ecologically minded. Never mind Save the Whale, Lizzie would have Save the Wasps; Save the Worms; Save the Weevil.)

Dad lowered his arms and glowered at Lizzie. "My dear child," he began, "I am about to begin the very difficult Spell of Merciful Release."

"Isn't that just another way of saying you're going to kill them?" Lizzie persisted.

"No, it is not," said Dad. "It means I am going to release them to go home. To trundle on their separate ways. Some to nice safe little havens under garden stones and flower pots. Some to graze on fine Wilton carpets. Some to nice damp coal sheds. Some to—"

"But how did Monika gather such an army of them?" I interrupted.

"Oh, really!" said Dad. "I sometimes wonder what they teach you at school. You must have heard of the Cry of the Woodlouse?"

I'm pleased to say that we *all* shook our heads.

"It is a tiny high-pitched cry that woodlice use when faced by danger or in great need. It is beyond human hearing, of course. The woodlouse often travels alone, but lives in a tribe. You've only to lift a garden stone to know this. When the Cry goes up, they all respond, loyal to a ... to a..."

"Louse," I finished for him.

"Exactly," said Dad. "Monika only had to give the Cry – becoming a woodlouse she'd know it automatically – and they came. In their thousands as it happens. Now if I have your combined approval, I'll begin." He raised his arms again.

There were a lot of words to the vamooshing Spell and I'm sure Dad added a few that weren't strictly necessary, a few he'd gathered on his travels to other centuries. He began in Latin. You could tell the Pin-stripes were impressed by that. And so were we.

"Chaos, rudis indigestaque moles.
Medio tutissimus ibis.
Video meliora, proboque.
Tempus edax rerum,"

chanted Dad. Later he told me what it meant. It was this:

Chaos, a rough and unordered mass.
(Meaning the woodlice.)
A middle course is the safest for you to take.
(Road directions.)
I see the better way, and approve it.
(Trust me.)
Time the devourer of everything.
(You better get going because you haven't got long.)

There was quite a lot of other stuff, but I rather lost track after that. I was still feeling very shaky from my ordeal, as Mum called it. And anyway, the woodlice simply stopped in their tracks at the very first words. Obviously they understood Latin. Very soon they formed into long lines of twos (like school crocodiles) and began going their different ways. The relief on the faces of the Pin-stripes was quite something to see.

There were so many woodlice that you could actually hear them as they trundled away down the marble stairs. We rushed to the window to watch them leaving. In the lights from the house we watched long, silvery-grey streams of them pouring under the door. We watched as they reformed into legions and set off again on different tracks, some heading towards the moors; some vanishing within the ivy surrounding a tree; a small group disappearing under a large stone near the gates of the house, all of them slowly vanishing into the darkness. And one of them – but which one – was Monika.

It was Lizzie who spotted her.

"There!" she cried, when all the other woodlice had disappeared. "She's on your sleeve! It must be her!"

I looked down at the pyjamas I was still wearing, and there she was. I lifted her gently on to my hand. She rolled on to her back and waved her legs at me in a very angry way. Hardly surprising really. I looked at Dad.

"Better put her on a chair," he said, "unless you want your hand broken. We'll all help you. We'll all think *Monika*."

There was a kind of collective growl from the Pin-stripes. Obviously they didn't want to think of Monika at all. She'd been the one to bring the plague of woodlice upon them.

"How can I 'think' her when I've never met her?" asked Lizzie's dad.

"You can just concentrate on her name," said Dad. "And a little quiet chanting of *Monika-Monika-Monika* wouldn't go amiss."

With everyone's help, it was easier than I expected. At first the woodlouse simply got fatter and fatter so that I thought it might explode, but slowly one booted leg emerged, then two and from the middle of the woodlouse Monika slowly straightened up, her ginger head popping out last. And there she was looking as she might if she'd just got out of bed, with her ginger hair standing on end. Shocked straight!

The first thing she said was, "Ants!"

"I'm terribly sorry," I said. "I don't know what went wrong. I was thinking *ant* terribly hard, but somehow that made me think of an army of ants, and army made me think of tanks and tanks made me think of—"

"I know," said Monika, "woodlice. And I can tell you it is an awfully hard life. Several times I landed on my back and thought I'd never get on my feet again. And it's all so slow!"

"That should teach you, Scully," said my dad, "that when doing the Changing Spell you must have perfect control of your thoughts."

"Yes, Dad," I said.

"But we have Monika to thank," Dad continued. "One more minute and you'd have been sieved, Scully. That would have been the end of your magic. It could have been the *universal* end of magic. With the Drop of Eternity, there'd be no stopping the Pin-stripes. They'd have sieved every trainee Wizard they could find – and there aren't many of you left."

"And we'd have made a fortune," I heard one of the Pin-stripes mutter.

"You've been a wonderful Minder," I said to Monika, "and an even better woodlouse!"

"Just you mind your cheek!" said Monika. "Or I might change into the sort of Minder that sets loads of homework."

"I would really like to get Scully home and into bed," said Mum.

"Can't we wait for the Outlandish Gentry to arrive?" I asked. "I want to see what they do with the Pin-stripes. And I've so many questions to ask. I don't know how any of you got here. I don't know how Lizzie and her father got involved. I don't know—"

"What I See," said Mum, trance-like again, "is a soft bed with a fresh duvet cover. I See a mug of cocoa and a plate of toast..."

Cocoa! Toast! I suddenly realized that I was terribly hungry and that it must be nearly midnight.

"I hear the gentle strains of Radio l," continued Mum, "and I see a trainee Wizard who is very, very tired."

"Absolutely right," said Dad, taking off his Wizard gear, folding it up and putting it back in its Tesco carrier bag. "There'll be plenty of time to answer all your questions, Scully. At home. As for the Outlandish Gentry and what they'll do with these Pin-stripes," Dad started walking all round them. "They might cook them of course. Or maybe turn them into robotic slaves." The Pin-stripes were all of a tremble again. "My guess," said Dad, "is that these rogues will very soon be doing an honest day's work. But we shall see. We shall certainly see."

WHAT MUM SAW

So that's how I came to be off school and tucked up in bed with everyone making a fuss of me. I've had plenty of time to practise my Dreaming – though my real night-time Dreaming has included quite a few nightmares. I think I've mastered the Changing Spell now, and besides, I haven't got the heart for it at the moment.

Also there's been time to talk to Mum, Dad and Lizzie and to find out just what happened after I was kidnapped – or was it Pin-striped – on my way to the market?

According to Mum, she was at the clock stall peacefully doing her knitting (for Wizards in reduced circumstances) when she had one of her Visions.

"I Saw a kind of strange laboratory lined with clocks," said Mum. "And men in white coats doing terrible experiments on Time."

"That's what he was wearing!" I cried. "The old man who nearly tricked Dad when he came to the market. The old man who stuck the needle in my arm."

"Don't keep interrupting," said Mum. "The next thing I saw was that they had taken our clock, our grandfather, and they were taking it apart, looking for something."

"So you knew then?"

"Yes, I knew what they were after. And I knew there was some danger. I didn't connect it to you. As you know, I never See any of us in my Visions."

"Shame," I said. "I wish you'd try harder."

"So," said Mum, ignoring this, "I thought the best thing I could do would be to remove the Drop of Eternity. I slid the phial out of the pendulum and hid it." Mum started to giggle.

"Where?" I asked.

"Between my boobs," said Mum. "The phial slid down there very neatly. Fitted perfectly."

"Then what?"

"Then nothing very much. Just about three o'clock I slipped off to the loo and to get a cup of tea.

"I asked Penny to look after the stall for me and when I got back she said, 'Oh the men have been to collect the clock.' 'What clock?' I said, though of course I knew at once. 'Why the grandfather,' she said. 'They had a piece of paper authorizing collection.' Well, it's easy to fake a receipt, isn't it?"

"So what did you do when you discovered they'd taken the clock?"

"I shut up the stall early and went home. I thought I'd better get in touch with your father fast. And it was nearly four o'clock by then. I thought you'd be home. I didn't know you'd be on the way to the market."

"Or that I'd never get there," I said.

"Nor that," agreed Mum.

"So how did you find out?"

"You've Lizzie to thank for that," said Mum. "A very nice girl, that Lizzie."

"I think so too," I said.

"No need to blush," said Mum.

Actually, I think without Lizzie I might very well be totally sieved by now.

Of course in my panic to get down to the market and warn Mum about the old man, I quite forgot I'd asked Lizzie to tea. Lizzie hung about a bit, waiting for me. That's when she saw Monika arguing with a man in a Mercedes and eventually being pushed – struggling and shouting – into the passenger seat.

"I thought it was her husband," Lizzie said. "I thought they were just having a row." When I didn't turn up, Lizzie decided I'd gone on home. So she made her own way to our house.

"I was trying to contact your dad," Mum

said. "I was working backwards through the centuries. I was a bit bothered that you weren't home yet, but I thought you'd stopped to chat to someone. When Lizzie appeared on the doorstep, I knew. I knew at once that something was wrong."

In a funny kind of way, you could say that Lizzie became my Minder then. I've thought, since all this happened, that perhaps we are all Minders of one sort or another, looking after each other as best we can and that you can Mind people in all sorts of different ways, little and large. I suppose too, that at that moment, Lizzie also became a kind of Seer.

"All sorts of things came together in my head," Lizzie told me, when she came to visit after school, which she did most days now. "The cat in the classroom, the old man I'd seen hanging around the school, Monika being pushed into the car and the way I knew, somehow, that you were different. I got a kind of red light in my head. I knew you were in danger."

And so did Mum when after an hour I was still not home and when she walked into the kitchen and found the Drop of Eternity had been stolen.

"I thought you said you'd put it between your boobs?"

"I did. But I wasn't going to keep it there,

was I? When I got home I put the phial down on the table and when next I looked—"

"Robbery," I said. "The Scorpion Squad."

"I'd left the back door open for you," said Mum. "It was just about the silliest thing I've ever done."

"Too true," I said.

"Almost as silly as Changing someone into a woodlouse instead of an ant," said Mum.

"Almost," I said.

By the time Mum had discovered the phial had been stolen Dad was back, all in a jumble it seems because he gets – not jet lag exactly, but century lag. Lizzie says that he and Mum had this perfectly extraordinary conversation.

"I heard thee call me from a distant shore." began Dad.

"Scully," said Mum, "and the clock. Both kidnapped."

"Woman, dost thou say my son, my dear young squire, hast been stolen from me?"

And so on. It was at this point that Lizzie decided to get *her* dad.

"Of course, I know there's a lot to be said for magic," said Lizzie, "but what we needed was action. Your mum was all for a Seeing session and your dad – well, apart from the fact that we couldn't work out what he was talking about, he was going at the pace of the twelfth century or something. And if there's one thing my dad *is* good at, it's an emergency."

Lizzie called him on her mobile. He was round in no time, apparently. Or in the time it took for Dad to come back into the twentieth century and for Mum to have done her Seeing. She concentrated on the clock to begin with and of course saw lots and lots of clocks – all the ones in the hall of the Pin-stripes' mansion. She tried to visualize Monika, but all she got – as you might expect – was a woodlouse.

Lizzie's dad made her go on trying until she could See the house and describe it. And eventually he snapped his fingers and said, "Got it! Heythorpe House – on the edge of the moor. Take us an hour. Let's go!"

The funny thing is that Lizzie's dad wasn't a bit fazed by all these strange goings-on. By then, of course, Mum and Dad had had to explain about Wizards and the importance of the clock, and how I was still a trainee etc. Lizzie's dad took it all in his stride. According to Lizzie, ever since her dad had lost a million or two on the stock market, he'd been a changed man. "It was as if money weighed him down," Lizzie said. "And when he lost a lot of it he kind of bobbed up again, like a Hallowe'en apple."

Quite a lot of people changed after that dreadful time with the Pin-stripes. Dad changed. He said he thought he was near retirement and he was going to make a single book of all the scraps of Ancient Knowledge he'd accumulated in a lifetime. This meant he wouldn't be going off in the Telepod on his Time Travels. And Mum decided to take fewer clients. So we all had more time together.

As for me, well I suppose it wasn't until I finally met the Outlandish Gentry that the real change happened.

TRAVEL BY TELEPOD

In the few days left before my OG Test, Dad spent a lot of time with me. We did the Changing Practice together. I'd gone right off ants – in fact insects of any kind. But I could do cat, rabbit, squirrel and tortoise. Tortoise was my favourite actually. It's a wonderful feeling being able to tuck your head inside your shell and then pop it out again. Very snug.

I wasn't quite so good at coming back into myself. Dad said I kept on making grunting noises and always ended up scrambling to my feet. I needed more acrobatic grace. Lizzie begged and pleaded to be allowed to watch but Dad said that was "unwise". "Very unwise." He wanted to do a spell of forgetting on Lizzie and her dad so that they would forget everything they knew. But they both said that if they promised never to tell anyone, would that do instead and Dad said yes.

For myself, I wanted to see Monika. I wanted to know if she was really all right after the Night of the Pin-stripes (as we came to call it in the family) and I wanted to thank her properly for her Minding. Also I was very curious about what it had felt like being a woodlouse and how she had managed to gather together such an army of them.

I kept asking Mum or Dad if I could go round to see her and they kept on saying no. There was always some reason or other. Monika was still resting. She'd particularly asked not to be disturbed. She was writing up her Minder's Report for the OG and so on. Despite all the practice, I was still nervous about the Test – about facing the Outlandish Gentry really. They would know things about me already, and none of them very good. Monika would have had to report on the trauma of the poor spider turned into a cat and they would certainly know about Monika being abandoned as a woodlouse.

The other thing that made me particularly nervous was that the Test took place at midnight. Also, although the letter from the Gentry gave a date and a time, it didn't give a place. Perhaps *finding* the Gentry was part of the test. Dad seemed to think this quite funny when I suggested it to him.

"There's no problem finding the OG,

Scully," he said. "We travel by Telepod."

So that's what we did. It was quite a stormy night. Mum insisted I take a travel pill first. We were both dressed up, Dad and I – Dad in his starry Hat and Cloak and me in my plain purple cloak and no hat. I didn't feel like laughing at Dad and his Hat any more.

Mum gave me a big hug and a kiss and said, "Good luck and good magic, Scully," then we went up to Dad's den. The Telepod was all set up ready, buzzing slightly and with a message on the screen. It said:

GENTRY GATHERING
WAIT FOR COMMAND

"What do we do when it comes?" I whispered to Dad. I don't know why I whispered. It was the wind howling outside and the trembling of my knees and the way the Telepod itself seemed to be tensed for take-off. I didn't feel at all sleepy, I can tell you. I felt very wide awake.

"I press the button," said Dad, and he pointed to a yellow knob I'd never noticed before.

Then the screen flashed again. This time the message said:

READY AND WAITING
ERASMUS (SCULLY) BROWNE
TO REPORT IN NOW
SALUTATIONS FROM THE GENTRY

"Salutations," I squeaked. "What are they?"

"Just the Gentry's way of saying 'hello'," said Dad, grinning. "It's going to be fine, Scully. Hold my hand. We're off!"

And we were! At first there was a sudden and terrible darkness and all I was aware of was Dad holding my hand while with the other he held on to his Hat. And then it was like being on an incredibly fast inter-city train. A train going so fast that the landscape whizzed by in a long misty blur with sudden sparkling lights as if we were passing through city after city. After that there was a last zoom of darkness. I had my eyes tightly closed during this. I opened them to a room in a castle and the six Wizards of the West Country Branch of the Outlandish Gentry waiting for me.

THE OG TEST

It's true that one of them had a white beard and looked about two hundred years old, but the rest of them looked nothing like I expected.

The youngest had dark curly hair, wore jeans and had his feet up on a stool. He had the nicest smile I've ever seen and it was he who came forward to greet us.

"Welcome, Erasmus," he said and gave a small bow to my father. Apart from the old Wizard, who I took to be the Chief, and the young, smiling one, there were four others. They looked to me like a group of eccentrics. One wore a long smock like painters used to wear; another had a multi-coloured patchwork waistcoat. They sat round a big oak table cluttered with books, papers, plates of half-eaten sandwiches and mugs – each with a name on.

The young Wizard gestured to a seat in front

of the table and I sat down. Dad was given a large armchair. The oldest Wizard (*Ahir* it said on his mug) was consulting a book. Every now and again he looked up at me and I had the uncomfortable feeling that the book contained a record of my doings so far. And probably Monika's report.

While we waited a servant came up with a large jug. He wore a long striped apron with the ribbons tied round his waist. He looked vaguely familiar. I looked round at Dad to see if he recognized him. Dad winked. "Pin-stripes" he mouthed at me and I realized it was. The Pin-stripe wouldn't look me in the eye. He set a small table beside me and a mug. I think it was wine he poured into it, though I can't be sure. Anyway, it tasted delicious and what pleased – and surprised – me most was that the mug had my name on it. *Scully* painted in black squiggly letters.

When I'd finished the drink and a second Pin-stripe had collected all the mugs and plates, Ahir banged on the table with what looked like an enormous egg-timer.

"Gentlemen of the Gentry," he said, "we are here to examine and hopefully to welcome a new member into this, the West Country Branch of the Outlandish Gentry. It is many years since we have welcomed such a one and we and the People-people have need of him."

Then he turned to me. "Erasmus," he said,

"you are aware that there are three classes of Wizard."

"Yes, sir," I said.

"And they are?"

"Past, Present and Future, sir," I said.

"Correct. Let us first hear you recite the Wizards' Two-way Code."

I took a deep breath and began. It came out in a bit of a gabble.

"A Wizard should care for the magic that is within and without. Within himself and without in the world. Never shall he use his Powers other than for the good and always shall he hold himself a part of two worlds, the world of magic and the everyday world of People-people to whose well-being his work shall be dedicated."

Ahir smiled at me. Despite his great age he had a very young smile. "Word perfect," he said. "Now about the Changing Skill…"

"Do we really need to test him on that?" asked the young Wizard. "I would have thought he had proved himself in that Art."

"You mean the Change of our Agent into a woodlouse," said Ahir.

"Not only that, sir," said the young Wizard, "but its result – the overthrow of the Scorpions. As an Order it could have been the end of us if the Scorpions had succeeded."

"Quite so," said Ahir, "and young Erasmus here is to be congratulated on that. Nevertheless, the actual Change was clumsily done. I should like to see if our trainee has become more proficient."

"I can do mouse or squirrel or tortoise, sir," I said eagerly.

"Tortoise, I think," said Ahir, "a creature I am particularly fond of."

So I did my tortoise Change, right then and there in front of them all. I began by curling myself up very tightly and lifting my shoulders up round my ears. In a moment I could feel the shell growing on my back and then I could pop my head out and look at them all.

There was much laughter.

The young Wizard tapped my shell with a teaspoon, and I pushed my head further and further upwards, threw the shell off my back as you might throw off a coat, and I was myself again.

"Gracefully done," said Ahir. "And if I were now to ask you to Change into a sparrow, could you do it?"

I'd never tried a bird before, but it was easy. Easy because I'd never been so happy before. Somehow, among the Wizards I felt two things – at home and myself. So it was nothing to soar up to the roof of the room and perch on a beam above Ahir's head. The flight was so lovely I was almost reluctant to Change back, but I know this is one of the dangers of Wizardry – being carried away – so when Ahir called, "Return!" I did so at once.

And that left the Flash. I didn't know it, but it's the Flash that decides which kind of Wizard you're going to be – Past, Present or Future. I suppose if I'd thought about it, I'd have known which sort I *wanted* to be, but somehow – perhaps from fear of disappointment – I didn't *let* myself know.

It is very hard to get a Flash when there are six important Wizards watching you. From the corner of my eye I could see Dad clenching his fists. He gave me a single nod as if to say, "You can do it, Scully." So I closed not just my eyes, but my mind. And I made that kind of clear clean space in my head that allows first the light and then the pictures.

I saw Monika. Monika dancing in her blue robe with her ginger hair bright as a sunset about her. Monika waving at me and blowing a kiss. And in the distance, at the top of a hill, another child waiting for her. Waiting for a Minder. I opened my eyes. I had to wipe them too, because I knew what the Flash meant.

"Well?" said Ahir. "Tell us your Seeing."

"Monika," I said. "I saw Monika – I mean your Agent, sir. She was waving goodbye. She's gone to be Minder to another child – or maybe another Wizard-in-waiting."

"You see truly," said Ahir. "And you have performed all the tasks set you. Kneel before me now."

So I knelt before Ahir, and all the other Wizards (including Dad) stood up. Ahir turned the enormous egg-timer upside down.

"Erasmus Scully Browne, you are now a member of the Outlandish Gentry, a Wizard of the Second Class, dedicated to the Present, sworn to keep our Two-way Code."

Then he put a cloak round my shoulders. I was pleased it wasn't like Dad's but was made of velvet stripes in wonderful reds and yellows.

A Pin-stripe was summoned to hand round more mugs of wine and all the Outlandish Gentry raised their mugs and said, "To Scully, Wizard Elect!"

A Wizard dedicated to the Present – that's just what I wanted. I didn't want to be stuck with a lot of Ancient Knowledge, like Dad. And I didn't want to be sent off to the Academy in the lonely north to consider the Future. I wanted to stay in the Present with People-people. And particularly people like Lizzie.

There's a lot of work to do if you're a Second Class Wizard – particularly encouraging people to discover their magic genes, their sense of wonder.

Since I've become a Wizard Elect I've been considering Miss Pugh. I went to see her at the end of term. I had three commendations and one gold star by then.

"We're very pleased with your progress,

Scully," said Miss Pugh. "Obviously Ms Brewer – Monika – helped you considerably."

"Yes," I said, "yes she did. A pity she had to go off like that."

"It is, isn't it," said Miss Pugh without looking at me, "but I think she was called away. Agency work I think she said. But she left you a message."

I opened the envelope Miss Pugh gave me. There was a single piece of blue paper inside. On it Monika had drawn a border of woodlice and in the middle she'd written:

MIND HOW YOU GO, SCULLY
AND MIND THE MAGIC!

Love,

Monika x

Miss Pugh watched me reading the letter. She was standing by the window and now she took up a small watering can and began watering the spider plant on the sill. I suddenly remembered how – what felt like moons ago – when Miss Pugh had called me into her office to tell me I was getting a Minder, I'd tried a little magic on that spider plant.

Miss Pugh put down the watering can, turned and smiled at me. "It's doing awfully well, don't you think, Scully?" she said.

"Quite magical, really."

Then she stood back and I saw that the spider plant was overflowing the sill with its fronds and blooming – blooming with roses!

SOMETHING RARE AND SPECIAL
Judy Allen

A moving and enthralling story by a Whitbread Award-winning author.

Following her parents' divorce, Lyn moves out of London with her mother to a house by the sea. At first, missing her old friends and city life, Lyn feels like a fish out of water. But then, down on the sands, she meets Bill Walker, who opens her eyes to a new world – and something rare and special…

"A sensitive story, rich with thoughtful atmosphere." *Junior Education*

MONKEY
Veronica Bennett

"Hey, Pritchard! Monkey-features! Monkey, monkey, monkey!"

By teenager Harry Pritchard's own admission, he's a dork. At school he's taunted and bullied by the vicious "Brigadier" Gerard Fox; at home he's weighed down by the chores his mother sets him – the worst of which is having to look after his irritating little sister, Emma. At least, that *was* the worst until Mum volunteers him to visit a severely disabled patient of hers, Simon Schofield, two evenings a week. She says it'll do him good. But how can being a helpless cripple's monkey help him end Brig's bullying? Or get him a part in the Drama Club play? Or win the attentions of beautiful Louise Harding, the girl of his dreams? Simon, though, turns out to be quite different from what Harry imagines and, after meeting him, Harry's life undergoes dramatic – and traumatic – changes!

Touching, perceptive and thought-provoking, Veronica Bennett's book is a first novel of outstanding assurance and quality.

LONE WOLF
Kristine L. Franklin

Three years ago, following a family tragedy, Perry Dubois and his dad left the city and moved to a remote cabin in the American woods. Here in wolf country, they lead a solitary life. Perry doesn't even go to school, spending much of his time with his dog, Rhonda, in the cave that's his secret hideout. Then Willow Pestalozzi and her large family move into the empty house nearby and Perry finds his world invaded. For Willow is full of questions – questions that remind Perry of everything he's tried so hard to forget. She wants to be friends, but Perry doesn't need anyone, does he? He's a loner like the wolf he hears howling in the woods. And yet there's something about the Pestalozzis, with their mess and noise and warmth, that draws him in…

Kristine L. Franklin's absorbing and touching story reveals how learning to laugh again also means being able, at last, to cry.

BADGER ON THE BARGE
Janni Howker

"This set of five stories, each concerned with a relationship between young and old, is quality stuff... Not to be missed." *The Times Educational Supplement*

These fine stories abound with absorbing situations and memorable characters. Meet cussed, rebellious Miss Brady, who lives with a badger on a barge; the reviled old shepherd Reicker; Sally Beck, topiary gardener with an extraordinary past; the reclusive Egg Man; proudly independent Jakey ... and the young people whose lives they profoundly affect.

Winner of the International Reading Association Children's Book Award. Shortlisted for the Whitbread Children's Novel Award and the Carnegie Medal.

MY LIFE AS A MOVIE HERO
Eric Johns

In times of crisis, Owen Royston Barron is a hero.

Well, in the interactive movies that run in his head he is. In real life he feels more like a worm. "Look after Mum," his dad said – and what did Owen do? He encouraged Mum to move in with slobby, loud-mouthed Frank. Now Owen is out on the street with his mum and wonders if he'll ever be able to get things straight. Will he always be two people – one inside, one outside? Can he ever redeem himself for what he's done? As absorbing and entertaining as the best screenplay, this is the story of Owen's struggle to bring the movie that is his life to a happy ending.

SO MUCH TO TELL YOU
John Marsden

Scarred, literally, by her past, Marina has withdrawn into silence.

She speaks to no one. But, set the task of writing a diary by her English teacher, she finds a way of expressing her thoughts and feelings and of exploring the traumatic events that have caused her distress. There is so much she has to say...

"Beautifully written... The heroine's perceptiveness, sense of humour and fairmindedness temper the tragedy and offer a splendid read."
The Times Educational Supplement

"A moving chronicle of personal recovery."
The Observer

JOHNNY CASANOVA
Jamie Rix

Johnny Worms is hot to trot, the unstoppable sex machine, Johnny Casanova... Well, so he believes. So when love's thunderbolt strikes in the form of Alison Mallinson or a beautiful vision in purple what can Johnny do? And is it his fault that Cyborg Girl, Deborah Smeeton, finds him irresistible?

"A genuinely funny book, sparklingly well-written." *The Independent*

"The first chapter had me laughing aloud at least three times." *The Scotsman*

MORE WALKER PAPERBACKS
For You to Enjoy